Waller Edmund

Poetical Works Of Edmond Waller Vol 2

Waller Edmund

Poetical Works Of Edmond Waller Vol 2

ISBN/EAN: 9783337103385

Printed in Europe, USA, Canada, Australia, Japan

Cover: Foto ©Andreas Hilbeck / pixelio.de

More available books at **www.hansebooks.com**

BELL'S EDITION.

The POETS of GREAT BRITAIN
COMPLETE FROM
CHAUCER to CHURCHILL.

WALLER VOLUME II.
Take heed, fair Eve! you do not make
Another tempter of this Snake.

M.Love del.   W.Sharp Sc.

Printed for John Bell near Exeter Exchange Strand London Nov. 15.th 1777.

THE
POETICAL WORKS

OF

EDMUND WALLER.

IN TWO VOLUMES.

FROM MR. FENTON'S QUARTO EDIT. 1729.

WITH

THE LIFE OF THE AUTHOR.

When WALLER, kindling with celestial rage,
View'd the bright Harley of that wond'ring age,
His pleasing pain he taught the lute to breathe;
The Graces sung, and wove his myrtle wreath····
His Muse, by Nature form'd to please the fair,
Or sing of heroes with majestic air,
To melting strains attun'd her voice, and strove
To waken all the tender powers of love.····
The florid and sublime, the grave and gay,
From WALLER's beams imbibe a purer ray.····
Maker and model of melodious verse!
Accept these votive honours at thy herse.   FENTON.

VOL. II.

EDINBURG:

AT THE Apollo Press, BY THE MARTINS.
Anno 1777.

THE
POETICAL WORKS
OF
EDMUND WALLER.
VOL. II.

CONTAINING HIS

EPISTLES,	EPITAPHS,
SONGS,	FRAGMENTS,
EPIGRAMS,	DIVINE POEMS,

&c. &c. &c.

Tho' poets may of infpiration boaft,
Their rage, ill-govern'd, in the clouds is loft.
He that proportion'd wonders can difclofe,
At once his fancy and his judgment fhows.
Chafte moral writing we may learn from hence,
Neglect of which no wit can recompenfe.—
  Well-founding verfes are the charm we ufe,
Heroic thoughts and virtue to infufe.
Things of deep fenfe we may in profe unfold,
But they move more in lofty numbers told :—
For rudeft minds with harmony were caught,
And civil life was by the Mufes taught.

POEM TO LORD ROSCOMMON.

EDINBURG:
AT THE Apollo Prefs, BY THE MARTINS
Anno 1777.

I.

TO THE KING,

ON HIS NAVY.

Where'er thy Navy spreads her canvass wings,
Homage to thee, and peace to all she brings:
The French and Spaniard, when thy flags appear,
Forget their hatred, and consent to fear.
So Jove from Ida did both hosts survey,   5
And when he pleas'd to thunder part the fray.
Ships heretofore in seas like fishes sped,
The mightiest still upon the smallest fed:
Thou on the deep imposest nobler laws,
And by that justice hast remov'd the cause   10
Of those rude tempests, which for rapine sent,
Too oft', alas! involv'd the innocent.
Now shall the Ocean, as thy Thames, be free
From both those fates of storms and piracy.
But we most happy, who can fear no force   15
But winged troops, or Pegasean horse.
'Tis not so hard for greedy foes to spoil
Another nation as to touch our soil.
Should Nature's self invade the world again,
And o'er the centre spread the liquid main,   20

Thy pow'r were fafe, and her deftructive hand
Would but enlarge the bounds of thy command :
Thy dreadful fleet would ftyle thee Lord of All,
And ride in triumph o'er the drowned ball ;
Thofe tow'rs of oak o'er fertile plains might go, 25
And vifit mountains where they once did grow.

The world's Reftorer once could not endure
That finifh'd Babel fhonld thofe men fecure
Whofe pride defign'd that fabric to have ftood
Above the reach of any fecond flood ;   . 30
To thee, his chofen, more indulgent, he
Dares truft fuch pow'r with fo much piety.   32

II.

TO THE QUEEN,

occafioned upon fight of

HER MAJESTY'S PICTURE.

Well fare the hand which to our humble fight
Prefents that beauty which the dazzling light
Of royal fplendour hides from weaker eyes,
And all accefs, fave by this art, denies.
Here only we have courage to behold   5
This beam of glory, here we dare unfold
In numbers thus the wonders we conceive :
The gracious image, feeming to give leave,
Propitious ftands, vouchfafing to be feen,
And by our Mufe faluted Mighty Queen,   10

In whom th' extremes of pow'r and beauty move,
The Queen of Britain, and the Queen of Love!
    As the bright fun (to which we owe no fight
Of equal glory to your beauty's light)
Is wifely plac'd in fo fublime a feat,   15
To' extend his light and moderate his heat ;   .
So, happy 'tis you move in fuch a fphere,
As your high Majefty with awful fear
In human breafts might qualify that fire,
Which kindled by thofe eyes had flamed high'r   20
Than when the fcorched world like hazard run
By the approach of the ill-guided fun.
    No other nymphs have title to men's hearts,
But as their meannefs larger hope imparts :
Your beauty more the fondeft lover moves   25
With admiration than his private loves ;
With admiration! for a pitch fo high
(Save facred Charles his) never love durft fly.
Heav'n that preferr'd a fceptre to your hand,
Favour'd our freedom more than your command : 30
Beauty had crown'd you, and you muft have been
The whole world's miftrefs, other than a Queen.
All had been rivals, and you might have fpar'd,
Or kill'd and tyranniz'd, without a guard.   .
No pow'r achiev'd, either by arms or birth,   35
Equals Love's empire both in heav'n and earth.
Such eyes as your's on Jove himfelf have thrown
As bright and fierce a lightning as his own :

Witnefs our Jove, prevented by their flame
In his fwift paffage to th' Hefperian dame :   40
When, like a lion, finding in his way
To fome intended fpoil a fairer prey,
The royal youth purfuing the report
Of beauty, found it in the Gallic court :
There public care with private paffion, fought   45
A doubtful combat in his noble thought :
Should he confefs His greatnefs and his love,
And the free faith bt your great brother* prove;
With his Achates † breaking thro' the cloud
Of that difguife which did their graces fhroud;   50
And mixing with thofe gallants at the ball,
Dance with the ladies, and outfhine them all;
Or on his journey o'er the mountains ride?——
So when the fair Leucothoe he efpy'd,
To check his fteeds impatient Phœbus earn'd,   55
Tho' all the world was in his courfe concern'd:
What may hereafter her meridian do,
Whofe dawning beauty warm'd his bofom fo?
Not fo divine a flame, fince deathlefs gods
Forbore to vifit the defil'd abodes   60
Of men, in any mortal breaft did burn;
Nor fhall, till Piety and they return.   62

* Lewis XIII. K. of France.   † D. of Buckingham.

III.

TO THE

QUEEN-MOTHER OF FRANCE,

UPON HER LANDING.

GREAT Queen of Europe! where thy offspring wears
All the chief crowns; where princes are thy heirs;
As welcome thou to sea-girt Britain's shore,
As erst Latona (who fair Cynthia bore)
To Delos was: here shines a nymph as bright,   5
By thee disclos'd, with like increase of light.
Why was her joy in Belgia confin'd?
Or why did you so much regard the wind?
Scarce could the ocean (tho' enrag'd) have tost
Thy sov'reign bark, but where th' obsequious coast 10
Pays tribute to thy bed. Rome's conqu'ring hand
More vanquish'd nations under her command
Never reduc'd. Glad Berecynthia so
Among her deathless progeny did go;
A wreath of tow'rs adorn'd her rev'rend head,   15
Mother of all that on ambrosia fed.
Thy god-like race must sway the age to come,
As she Olympus peopled with her womb.
  Would those commanders of mankind obey
Their honour'd parent, all pretences lay   20
Down at your royal feet, compose their jars,
And on the growing Turk discharge these wars,

A iij

The Chriſtian knights that ſacred tomb ſhould wreſt
From Pagan hands, and triumph o'er the Eaſt :
Our England's Prince, and Gallia's Dolphin, might
Like young Rinaldo and Tancredi fight :   26
In ſingle combat by their ſwords again
The proud Argantes and fierce Soldan ſlain :
Again might we their valiant deeds recite,
And with your Tuſcan Muſe * exalt the fight.   30

IV.

THE COUNTRY,

TO MY LADY OF CARLISLE.

MADAM, of all the ſacred Muſe inſpir'd,
Orpheus alone could with the woods comply;
Their rude inhabitants his ſong admir'd,
And Nature's ſelf, in thoſe that could not lie :
Your Beauty next our ſolitude invades,   5
And warms us, ſhining thro' the thickeſt ſhades.

Nor ought the tribute which the wond'ring court
Pays your fair eyes, prevail with you to ſcorn
The anſwer and conſent to that report
Which, echo-like, the country does return :   10
Mirrors are taught to flatter, but our ſprings
Preſent th' impartial images of things.

A rural judge † diſpos'd of beauty's prize ;
A ſimple ſhepherd † was preferr'd to Jove

                    * Taſſo.   † Paris.

Down to the mountains from the partial skies, 15
Came Juno, Pallas, and the Queen of Love,
To plead for that which was so justly giv'n
To the bright Carlisle of the court of heav'n.

Carlisle! a name which all our woods are taught
Loud as their Amaryllis to refound : 20
Carlisle! a name which on the bark is wrought
Of every tree that's worthy of the wound.
From Phœbus' rage our shadows and our streams
May guard us better than from Carlisle's beams. 24

V.

TO PHYLLIS.

Phyllis! 'twas love that injur'd you,
And on that rock your Thyrsis threw,
Who for proud Cælia could have dy'd,
While you no less accus'd his pride.
   Fond Love his darts at random throws, 5
And nothing springs from what he sows :
From foes discharg'd as often meet
The shining points of arrows fleet,
In the wide air creating fire,
As souls that join in one desire. 10
   Love made the lovely Venus burn
In vain, and for the cold youth * mourn,

     * Adonis.

Who the purfuit of churlifh beafts
Preferr'd to fleeping on her breafts.
    Love makes fo many hearts the prize   15
Of the bright Carlifle's conqu'ring eyes,
Which fhe regards no more than they
The tears of leffer beauties weigh.
So have I feen the lofl clouds pour
Into the fea an ufelefs fhow'r,   20
And the vex'd failors curfe the rain,
For which poor fhepherds pray'd in vain.
    Then, Phyllis, fince our paffions are
Govern'd by chance, and not the care,
But fport of Heav'n, which takes delight   25
To look upon this Parthian fight
Of Love, ftill flying, or in chafe,
Never encount'ring face to face,
No more to Love we'll facrifice,
But to the beft of deities;   30
And let our hearts, which Love disjoin'd,
By his kind mother be combin'd.   32

VI.

TO MY

LORD OF NORTHUMBERLAND,

UPON THE DEATH OF HIS LADY.

To this great lofs a fea of tears is due,
But the whole debt not to be paid by you:

2

Charge not yourfelf with all, nor render vain
Thofe show'rs the eyes of us your fervants rain.
Shall grief contract the largenefs of that heart   5
In which nor fear nor anger has a part?
Virtue would blush if time should boaft (which dries
Her fole child dead, the tender mother's eyes)
Your mind's relief, where reafon triumphs fo
Over all paffions, that they ne'er could grow   10
Beyond their limits in your noble breaft,
To harm another, or impeach your reft.
This we obferv'd, delighting to obey
One who did never from his great felf ftray;
Whofe mild example feemed to engage   15
Th' obfequious feas, and teach them not to rage.

    The brave Æmilius, his great charge laid down,
(The force of Rome, and fate of Macedon)
In his loft fons did feel the cruel ftroke
Of changing fortune, and thus highly fpoke   20
Before Rome's people; "We did oft' implore,
" That if the Heav'ns had any bad in ftore
" For your Æmilius, they would pour that ill
" On his own houfe, and let you flourish ftill."
You on the barren feas, my Lord, have fpent   25
Whole fprings, and fummers to the public lent;
Sufpended all the pleasures of your life,
And shorten'd the short joy of fuch a wife;
For which your country's more obliged than
For many lives of old lefs happy men.   30

You that have sacrific'd so great a part
Of youth, and private bliss, ought to impart
Your sorrow too, and give your friends a right
As well in your affliction as delight.
Then with Æmilian courage bear this cross,   35
Since public persons only public loss
Ought to affect. And tho' her form and youth,
Her application to your will and truth,
That noble sweetness, and that humble state,
(All snatch'd away by such a hasty fate!) .   40
Might give excuse to any common breast,
With the huge weight of so just grief opprest;
Yet let no portion of your life be stain'd
With passion, but your character maintain'd
To the last act. It is enough her stone   45
May honour'd be with superscription
Of the sole lady who had pow'r to move
The great Northumberland to grieve and love.   48

VII.

TO MY LORD ADMIRAL,

OF HIS LATE SICKNESS AND RECOVERY.

WITH joy like ours the Thracian youth invades
Orpheus, returning from th' Elysian shades;
Embrace the hero, and his stay implore;
Make it their public suit he would no more

Defert them fo, and for his fpoufe's fake,   5
His vanifh'd love, tempt the Lethean lake.
The ladies, too, the brighteft of that time,
(Ambitious all his lofty bed to climb)
Their doubtful hopes with expectation feed,
Who fhall the fair Eurydice fucceed :   10
Eurydice! for whom his num'rous moan
Makes lift'ning trees and favage mountains groan :
Thro' all the air his founding ftrings dilate
Sorrow like that which touch'd our hearts of late.
Your pining ficknefs, and your reftlefs pain,   15
At once the land affecting and the main,
When the glad news that you were Admiral
Scarce thro' the nation fpread, 'twas fear'd by all
That our great Charles, whofe wifdom fhines in you,
Would be perplexed how to chufe a new.   20
So more than private was the joy and grief,
That at the worft it gave our fouls relief,
That in our age fuch fenfe of virtue liv'd,
They joy'd fo juftly, and fo juftly griev'd.
Nature (her faireft lights eclipfed) feems   25
Herfelf to fuffer in thofe fharp extremes;
While not from thine alone thy blood retires,
But from thofe cheeks which all the world admires.
The ftem thus threaten'd, and the fap in thee,
Droop all the branches of that noble tree!   30
Their beauty they, and we our love fufpend;
Nought can our wifhes fave thy health intend.

As lilies overcharg'd with rain, they bend
Their beauteous heads, and with high heav'n contend;
Fold thee within their snowy arms, and cry   35
He is too faultless and too young to die.
So like immortals round about thee they
Sit, that they fright approaching Death away.
Who would not languish, by so fair a train
To be lamented and restor'd again?   40
Or, thus with-held, what hasty soul would go,
Tho' to the blest? O'er young Adonis so
Fair Venus mourn'd, and with the precious show'r
Of her warm tears cherish'd the springing flow'r.

   The next support, fair hope of your great name, 45
And second pillar of that noble frame,
By loss of thee would no advantage have,
But step by step pursue thee to the grave.

   And now relentless Fate, about to end
The line which backward does so far extend   50
That antique stock, which still the world supplies
With harvest spirits and with brightest eyes,
Kind Phœbus, interposing, bid me say,
Such storms no more shall shake that house; but they,
Like Neptune, and his sea-born niece *, shall be 55
The shining glories of the land and sea;
With courage guard, and beauty warm, our age,
And lovers fill with like poetic rage.   58

* Venus.

VIII.

TO VAN DYCK.

RARE Artifan! whofe pencil moves
Not our delights alone, but loves;
From thy fhop of Beauty we
Slaves return'd that enter'd free.
The heedlefs lover does not know
Whofe eyes they are that wound him fo;
But, confounded with thy art,
Inquires her name that has his heart.
Another, who did long refrain,
Feels his old wound bleed frefh again   10
With dear remembrance of that face,
Where now he reads new hope of grace:
Nor fcorn nor cruelty does find,
But gladly fuffers a falfe wind
To blow the afhes of defpair   15
From the reviving brand of care.
Fool! that forgets her ftubborn look
This foftnefs from thy finger took.
Strange! that thy hand fhould not infpire
The beauty only, but the fire: 20
Not the form alone, and grace,
But act and power of a face.
May'ft thou yet thyfelf as well,
As all the world befides, excel!

Volume II.   B

So you the unfeign'd truth rehearfe,   25
(That I may make it live in verfe)
Why thou couldft not at one affay,
That face to after-times convey,
Which this admires.   Was it thy wit
To make her oft' before thee fit ?   30
Confefs, and we'll forgive thee this;
For who would not repeat that blifs ?
And frequent fight of fuch a dame
Buy with the hazard of his fame ?
Yet who can tax thy blamelefs fkill,   35
'Tho' thy good hand had failed ftill,·
When Nature's felf fo often errs ?
She for this many thoufand years
Seems to have practis'd with much care,
To frame the race of women fair ;   40
Yet never could a perfect birth
Produce before to grace the earth,
Which waxed old ere it could fee
Her that amaz'd thy art and thee.

    But now 'tis done, O let me know   45
Where thofe immortal colours grow
That could this deathlefs piece compofe !
In lilies ? or the fading rofe ?
No; for this theft thou haft climb'd high'r
Than did Prometheus for his fire.   50

IX.

TO MY LORD OF LEICESTER.

NOT that thy trees at Penſhurſt groan,
Oppreſſed with their timely load,
And ſeem to make their ſilent moan,
That their great Lord is now abroad :
They to delight his taſte or eye   5
Would ſpend themſelves in fruit, and die.

Not that thy harmleſs deer repine,
And think themſelves unjuſtly ſlain
By any other hand than thine,
Whoſe arrows they would gladly ſtain ;   10
No, nor thy friends, which hold too dear
That peace with France which keeps thee there.

All theſe are leſs than that great cauſe
Which now exacts your preſence here,
Wherein there meet the divers laws   15
Of public and domeſtic care.
For one bright nymph our youth contends,
And on your prudent choice depends.

Not the bright ſhield of Thetis' ſon *,
(For which ſuch ſtern debate did riſe,   20

* Achilles.

B ij

That the great Ajax Telamon
Refus'd to live without the prize)
Those Achive peers did more engage,
Than she the gallants of our age.

That beam of beauty which begun   25
To warm us so when thou wert here,
Now scorches like the raging sun,
When Sirius does first appear.
O fix this flame! and let despair
Redeem the rest from endless care.   30

X.

TO MRS. BRAUGHTON,

SERVANT TO SACHARISSA.

FAIR Fellow-servant! may your gentle ear
Prove more propitious to my slighted care
Than the bright dame's we serve: for her relief
(Vex'd with the long expressions of my grief)
Receive these plaints; nor will her high disdain   5
Forbid by humble Muse to court her train.
    So, in those nations which the sun adore,
Some modest Persian, or some weak-ey'd Moor,
No higher dares advance his dazzled sight,
Than to some gilded cloud, which near the light   10
Of their ascending god adorns the East,
And, graced with his beams, outshines the rest.

Thy skilful hand contributes to our woe,
And whets those arrows which confound us so.
A thousand Cupids in those curls do sit   15
(Those curious nets!) thy slender fingers knit.
The Graces put not more exactly on
Th' attire of Venus when the Ball she won,
Than Sacharissa by thy care is drest,
When all our youth prefers her to the rest.   20
    You the soft season know when best her mind
May be to pity or to love inclin'd:
In some well-chosen hour supply his fear,
Whose hopeless love durst never tempt the ear
Of that stern goddess. You, her priest, declare   25
What off'rings may propitiate the fair:
Rich orient pearl, bright stones that ne'er decay,
Or polish'd lines, which longer last than they:
For if I thought she took delight in those,
To where the cheerful Morn does first disclose,   30
(The shady Night removing with her beams)
Wing'd with bold love I'd fly to fetch such gems.
But since her eyes, her teeth, her lip, excels
All that is found in mines or fishes' shells,
Her nobler part as far exceeding these,   35
None but immortal gifts her mind should please.
The shining jewels Greece and Troy bestow'd
On Sparta's Queen *, her lovely neck did load,
And snowy wrists; but when the town was burn'd,
Those fading glories were to ashes turn'd: 40

* Helen.   B iij

Her beauty, too, had perish'd, and her fame,
Had not the Muse redeem'd them from the flame. 42

XI.

TO MY YOUNG LADY LUCY SIDNEY.

WHY came I so untimely forth
Into a world which, wanting thee,
Could entertain us with no worth
Or shadow of felicity?
That time should me so far remove　　　　　5
From that which I was born to love!

Yet, fairest Blossom! do not slight
That age which you may know so soon:
The rosy Morn resigns her light
And milder glory to the Noon:　　　　　10
And then what wonders shall you do,
Whose dawning beauty warms us so?

Hope waits upon the flow'ry prime;
And summer, tho' it be less gay,
Yet is not look'd on as a time　　　　　15
Of declination or decay:
For with a full hand that does bring
All that was promis'd by the spring.　　　　　18

XII.

TO AMORET,

Fair! that you may truly know
What you unto Thyrfis owe,
I will tell you how I do
Sachariffa love and you.

Joy falutes me when I fet   5
My bleft eyes on Amoret;
But with wonder I am ftrook,
While I on the other look.

If fweet Amoret complains,
I have fenfe of all her pains;   10
But for Sachariffa I
Do not only grieve, but die.

All that of myfelf is mine,
Lovely Amoret! is thine:
Sachariffa's captive fain   15
Would untie his iron chain,
And thofe fcorching beams to fhun,
To thy gentle fhadow run.

If the foul had free election
To difpofe of her affection,   20
I would not thus long have borne
Haughty Sachariffa's fcorn:
But 'tis fure fome pow'r above,
Which controls our wills in love!

If not a love, a ſtrong deſire   25
To create and ſpread that fire
In my breaſt, ſolicits me,
Beauteous Amoret! for thee.

   'Tis amazement more than love,
Which her radiant eyes do move: 30
If leſs ſplendour wait on thine,
Yet they ſo benignly ſhine,
I would turn my dazzled ſight
To behold their milder light:
But as hard 'tis to deſtroy   35
That high flame, as to enjoy;
Which how eas'ly I may do,
Heav'n (as eas'ly ſcal'd) does know!

   Amoret! as ſweet and good
As the moſt delicious food,   40
Which but taſted does impart
Life and gladneſs to the heart.

   Sachariſſa's beauty 's wine,
Which to madneſs doth incline;
Such a liquor as no brain   45
That is mortal can ſuſtain.

   Scarce can I to Heav'n excuſe
The devotion which I uſe
Unto that adored dame;
For 'tis not unlike the ſame   50
Which I thither ought to ſend;
So that if it could take end,

It would to Heav'n itſelf be due,
To ſucceed her and not you;
Who already have of me   55
All that's not idolatry;
Which, tho' not ſo fierce a flame,
Is longer like to be the ſame.
　　Then ſmile on me, and I will prove
Wonder is ſhorter-liv'd than love.   60

<h2>XIII.</h2>

<h2>TO AMORET.</h2>

Amoret! the Milky Way
Fram'd of many nameleſs ſtars!
The ſmooth ſtream where none can ſay
He this drop to that prefers!

Amoret! my lovely Foe!   5
Tell me where thy ſtrength does lie?
Where the pow'r that charms us ſo;
In thy ſoul, or in thy eye?

By that ſnowy neck alone,
Or thy grace in motion ſeen,   10
No ſuch wonders could be done;
Yet thy waiſt is ſtraight and clean
As Cupid's ſhaft, or Hermes' rod,
And pow'rful, too, as either god.   14

XIV.

TO PHYLLIS.

Phyllis! why should we delay
Pleasures shorter than the day?
Could we (which we never can)
Stretch our lives beyond their span,
Beauty like a shadow flies,   5
And our youth before us dies.
Or would youth and beauty stay,
Love hath wings, and will away.
Love hath swifter wings than Time.
Change in love to Heav'n does climb.   10
Gods, that never change their state,
Vary oft' their love and hate.
    Phyllis! to this truth we owe
All the love betwixt us two.
Let not you and I inquire   15
What has been our past desire;
On what shepherds you have smil'd,
Or what nymphs I have beguil'd:
Leave it to the planets too,
What we shall hereafter do;   20
For the joys we now may prove,
Take advice of present love.   22

XV.

TO MY LORD OF FALKLAND.

Brave Holland leads, and with him Falkland goes:
Who hears this told, and does not straight suppose
We send the Graces and the Muses forth,
To civilize and to instruct the North?
Not that these ornaments make swords less sharp; 5
Apollo bears as well his bow as harp:
And tho' he be the patron of that spring,
Where, in calm peace, the sacred virgins sing,
He courage had to guard th' invaded throne
Of Jove, and cast the ambitious giants down.   10
    Ah, noble Friend! with what impatience all
That know thy worth, and know how prodigal
Of thy great soul thou art, (longing to twist
Bays with that ivy which so early kiss'd
Thy youthful temples) with what horror we   15
Think on the blind events of war and thee?
To fate exposing that all-knowing breast
Among the throng, as cheaply as the rest;
Where oaks and brambles (if the copse be burn'd)
Confounded lie, to the same ashes turn'd.   20
    Some happy wind over the ocean blow
This tempest yet, which frights our island so!
Guarded with ships, and all the sea our own,
From Heav'n this mischief on our heads is thrown.

In a late dream the Genius of this land,   25
Amaz'd, I faw, like the fair Hebrew *, ftand,
When firft fhe felt the twins begin to jar,
And found her womb the feat of Civil war.
Inclin'd to whofe relief, and with prefage
Of better fortune for the prefent age,   30
Heav'n fends, quoth I, this difcord for our good,
To warm, perhaps, but not to wafte our blood;
To raife our drooping fpirits, grown the fcorn
Of our proud neighbours, who ere long fhall mourn
(Tho' now they joy in our expected harms)   35
We had occafion to refume our arms.

A lion fo with felf-provoking fmart,
(His rebel tall fcourging his nobler part)
Calls up his courage, then begins to roar,
And charge his focs, who thought him mad before. 40

XVI.

TO A LADY,

SINGING A SONG OF HIS COMPOSING.

CHLORIS! yourfelf you fo excel,
When you vouchfafe to breathe my thought,
That, like a fpirit, with this fpell
Of my own teaching, I am caught.

That eagle's fate and mine are one,   5
Which, on the fhaft that made him die,

---

* Rebekah.

3

Efpy'd a feather of his own,
Wherewith he wont to foar fo high.

Had Echo, with fo fweet a grace,
Narciffus' loud complaints return'd,   10
Not for reflection of his face,
But of his voice, the boy had burn'd.   12

XVII.

TO THE MUTABLE FAIR.

Here, Cælia! for thy fake I part
With all that grew fo near my heart;
The paffion that I had for thee,
The faith, the love, the conftancy!
And, that I may fuccefsful prove,   5
Transform myfelf to what you love.
    Fool that I was! fo much to prize
Thofe fimple virtues you defpife:
Fool! that with fuch dull arrows ftrove,
Or hop'd to reach a flying dove: 10
For you, that are in motion ftill,
Decline our force, and mock our fkill;
Who, like Don Quixote, do advance
Againft a windmill our vain lance.
    Now will I wander thro' the air,   15
Mount, make a ftoop at ev'ry fair;
And, with a fancy unconfin'd,
(As lawlefs as the fea or wind)

Purfue you wherefoe'er you fly,
And with your various thoughts comply.
   The formal ftars do travel fo,
As we their names and courfes know;
And he that on their changes looks,
Would think them govern'd by our books;
But never were the clouds reduc'd
To any art : the motion us'd
By thofe free vapours are fo light,
So frequent, that the conquer'd fight
Defpairs to find the rules that guide
Thofe gilded fhadows as they flide;
And therefore of the fpacious air
Jove's royal confort had the care;
And by that pow'r did once efcape,
Declining bold Ixion's rape :
She, with her own refemblance, grac'd
A fhining cloud, which he embrac'd.
   Such was that image, fo it fmil'd
With feeming kindnefs, which beguil'd
Your Thyrfis lately, when he thought
He had his fleeting Cælia caught.
'Twas fhap'd like her, but for the fair,
He fill'd his arms with yielding air.
   A fate for which he grieves the lefs,
Becaufe the gods had like fuccefs :
For in their ftory one, we fee,
Purfues a nymph, and takes a tree;

A fecond, with a lover's hafte,
Soon overtakes whom he had chas'd;
But fhe that did a virgin feem,
Poffefs'd, appears a wand'ring ftream.
For his fuppofed love, a third
Lays greedy hold upon a bird,
And ftands amaz'd to find his dear.
A wild inhabitant of th' air.
To thefe old tales fuch nymphs as you
Give credit, and ftill make them new;
The am'rous now like wonders find
In the fwift changes of your mind.

But, Cælia, if you apprehend
The Mufe of your incenfed friend,
Nor would that he record your blame,
And make it live, repeat the fame;
Again deceive him, and again,
And then he fwears he'll not complain:
For ftill to be deluded fo,
Is all the pleafure lovers know;
Who, like good falc'ners, take delight
Not in the quarry, but the flight.

XVIII.

TO A LADY,

FROM WHOM HE RECEIVED A SILVER PEN.

MADAM! intending to have try'd
The filver favour which you gave,

In ink the fhining point I dy'd,
And drench'd it in the fable wave;
When, griev'd to be fo foully ftain'd,   5
On you it thus to me complain'd.

" Suppofe you had deferv'd to take
From her fair hand fo fair a boon,
Yet how deferved I to make
So ill a change; who ever won   10
Immortal praife for what I wrote,
Inftructed by her noble thought?

I, that expreffed her commands
To mighty lords and princely dames,
Always moft welcome to their hands,   15
Proud that I would record their names,.
Muft now be taught an humble ftyle,
Some meaner beauty to beguile!"

So I, the wronged pen to pleafe,
Make it my humble thanks exprefs   20
Unto your Ladyfhip in thefe:
And now 'tis forced to confefs
That your great felf did ne'er indite,
Nor that, to one more noble, write.   24

XIX.

TO CHLORIS.

CHLORIS! fince firft our calm of peace
Was frighted hence, this good we find,
Your favours with your fears increafe,
And growing mifchiefs make you kind.

So the fair tree, which ftill preferves
Her fruit and ftate while no wind blows,
In ftorms from that uprightnefs fwerves,
And the glad earth about her ftrows
With treafure, from her yielding bows.

XX.

TO A LADY IN RETIREMENT.

SEES not my love how Time refumes
The glory which he lent thefe flow'rs?
Tho' none fhould tafte of their perfumes,
Yet muft they live but fome few hours.
Time what we forbear devours!

Had Helen, or the Egyptian Queen *,
Been near fo thrifty of their graces,
Thofe beauties muft at length have been
The fpoil of Age, which finds out faces
In the moft retired places.

* Cleopatra.

C iij

Should fome malignant planet bring
A barren drought or ceafelefs fhow'r
Upon the autumn or the fpring,
And fpare us neither fruit nor flow'r,
Winter would not flay an hour.   15

Could the refolve of love's neglect
Preferve you from the violation
Of coming years, then more refpect
Were due to fo divine a fafhion,
Nor would I indulge my paffion.   20

XXI.

TO MR. GEORGE SANDYS,

on his tranflation

OF SOME PARTS OF THE BIBLE.

How bold a work attempts that pen,
Which would enrich our vulgar tongue
With the high raptures of thofe men
Who here with the fame fpirit fung
Wherewith they now affift the choir   5
Of angels, who their fongs admire!

What ever thofe infpired fouls
Were urged to exprefs, did fhake
The aged Deep, and both the poles;
Their num'rous thunder could awake   10

Dull Earth, which does with Heav'n confent
To all they wrote, and all they meant.

Say, facred Bard! what could beftow
Courage on thee to foar fo high?
Tell me, brave Friend! what help'd thee fo   15
To fhake off all mortality?
To light this torch thou haft climb'd high'r
Than he who ftole celeftial fire *.   18

XXII.

TO MR. WILLIAM LAWES,

Who had then newly fet a fong of mine, in the'year 1635.

Verse makes heroic virtue live,
But you can life to verfes give.
As when in open air we blow,
The breath, (tho' ftrain'd) founds flat and low,
But if a trumpet take the blaft,   5
It lifts it high, and makes it laft:
So in your airs our numbers dreft,
Make a fhrill fally from the breaft
Of nymphs, who finging what we penn'd,
Our paffions to themfelves commend;   10
While love, victorious with thy art,
Governs at once their voice and heart.

* Prometheus.

You by the help of tune and time,
Can make that song which was but rhyme.
Noy pleading, no man doubts the caufe,   15
Or queftions verfes fet by Lawes.

 As a church-window, thick with paint,
Lets in a light but dim and faint;
So others with divifion hide
The light of fenfe, the poet's pride;   20
But you alone may truly boaft
That not a fyllable is loft:
The writer's and the fetter's fkill
At once the ravifh'd ears do fill.
Let thofe which only warble long,   25
And gargle in their throats a fong,
Content themfelves with *Ut, Re, Mi:*
Let words and fenfe be fet by thee.   28

XXIII.

TO SIR WILLIAM D'AVENANT,

UPON HIS TWO FIRST BOOKS OF GONDIBERT.

Written in France.

Thus the wife nightingale that leaves her home,
Her native wood, when ftorms and winter come,
Purfuing conftantly the cheerful fpring,
To foreign groves does her old mufic bring.

The drooping Hebrews banifh'd, harps unftrung, 5
At Babylon upon the willows hung:
Your's founds aloud, and tells us you excel
No lefs in courage than in finging well:
While unconcern'd you let your country know,
They have impoverifh'd themfelves, not you; . 10
Who with the Mufes' help can mock thofe fates
Which threaten kingdoms and diforder ftates.
So Ovid, when from Cæfar's rage he fled, ·
The Roman Mufe to Pontus with him led;
Where he fo fung, that we, thro' Pity's glafs, 15
See Nero milder than Auguftus was.
Hereafter fuch in thy behalf fhall be
Th' indulgent cenfure of pofterity.
To banifh thofe who with fuch art can fing,
Is a rude crime which its own curfe doth bring: 20
Ages to come fhall ne'er know how they fought,
Nor how to love their prefent youth be taught.
This to thyfelf.——Now to thy matchlefs book,
Wherein thofe few that can with judgment look,
May find old love in pure frefh language told, 25
Like new-ftamp'd coin made out of angel gold;
Such truth in love as th' antique world did know, ·
In fuch a ftyle as courts may boaft of now;
Which no bold tales of gods or monfters fwell,
But human paffions, fuch as with us dwell. 30
Man is thy theme, his virtue or his rage
Drawn to the life in each elab'rate page. · ·

Mars nor Bellona are not named here,
But such a Gondibert as both might fear :
Venus had here, and Hebe, been 'out'shin'd
By thy bright Birtha and thy Rhodalind.
Snch is thy happy skill, and such the odds
Betwixt thy worthies and the Grecian gods!
Whose deities in vain had here come down,
Where mortal beauty wears the sov'reign crown :
Such as of flesh compos'd, by flesh and blood,
Tho' not resisted, may be understood.

XXIV.

TO MY

WORTHY FRIEND MR. WASE,

THE TRANSLATOR OF GRATIUS.

Thus by the music we may know,
When noble wits a-hunting go
Thro' groves that on Parnassus grow.

The Muses all the chase adorn;
My friend on Pegasus is borne;
And young Apollo winds the horn.

Having old Gratius in the wind,
No pack of critics e'er could find,
Or he know more of his own mind.

Here huntfmen with delight may read   10
How to chufe dogs for fcent or fpeed,
And how to change or mend the breed.

What arms to ufe, or nets to frame,
Wild beafts to combat or to tame;
With all the myft'ries of that game.   15

But, worthy Friend! the face of war
In ancient times doth differ far
From what our fiery battles are.

Nor is it like, fince powder known,
'That man, fo cruel to his own,   20
Should fpare the race of beafts alone.

No quarter now, but with the gun
Men wait in trees from fun to fun,
And all is in a moment done.

And therefore we expect your next   25
Should be no comment, but a text
To tell how modern beafts are vext.

Thus would I further yet engage
Your gentle Mufe to court the age
With fomewhat of your proper rage;   30

Since none does more to Phœbus owe,
Or in more languages can show
Those arts which you so early know.   33

XXV.

TO HIS

WORTHY FRIEND MR. EVELYN,

UPON HIS TRANSLATION OF LUCRETIUS.

Lucretius, (with a stork-like fate,
Born and translated in a state)
Comes to proclaim, in English verse,
No monarch rules the universe,
But chance, and atoms, make this All   5
In order democratical,
Where bodies freely run their course,
Without design, or fate, or force :
And this in such a strain he sings,
As if his Muse, with angels' wings,   10
Had soar'd beyond our utmost sphere,
And other worlds discover'd there :
For his immortal, boundless wit,
To Nature does no bounds permit,
But boldly has remov'd those bars   15
Of heav'n, and earth, and seas, and stars,
By which they were before suppos'd,
By narrow wits, to be inclos'd,

Till his free Mufe threw down the pale,
And did at once difpark them all.   20
   So vaft this argument did feem,
That the wife author did efteem
The Roman language (which was fpread
O'er the whole world, in triumph led)
A tongue too narrow to unfold   25
The wonders which he would have told.
This fpeaks thy glory, noble Friend!
And Britifh language does commend ;
For here Lucretius whole we find,
His words, his mufic, and his mind.   30
Thy art has to our country brought
All that he writ, and all he thought.
Ovid tranflated, Virgil too,
Shew'd long fince what our tongue could do :
Nor Lucan we, nor Horace fpar'd ;   35
Only Lucretius was too hard :
Lucretius, like a fort, did ftand
Untouch'd, till your victorious hand
Did from his head this garland bear,
Which now upon your own you wear :   40
A garland! made of fuch new bays,
And fought in fuch untrodden ways,
As no man's temples e'er did crown,
Save this great author's and your own!   44

XXVI.

TO HIS

WORTHY FRIEND SIR THO. HIGGONS,

upon his translation of

THE VENETIAN TRIUMPH.

THE winged Lion's * not so fierce in fight,
As Liberi's hand presents him to our sight;
Nor would his pencil make him half so fierce,
Or roar so loud, as Businello's verse:
But your translation does all three excel,   5
The fight, the piece, and lofty Businel.
As their small gallies may not hold compare
With our tall ships, whose sails employ more air;
So does the Italian to your genius vail,
Mov'd with a fuller and a nobler gale.   10
Thus while your Muse spreads the Venetian story,
You make all Europe emulate her glory:
You make them blush weak Venice should defend
The cause of Heav'n, while they for words contend;
Shed Christian blood, and pop'lous cities safe,   15
Because they 're taught to use some diff'rent phrase.
If, list'ning to your charms, we could our jars
Compose, and on the Turk discharge these wars,
Our British arms the sacred tomb might wrest
From Pagan hands, and triumph o'er the East;   20

     * The arms of Venice.

And then you might our own high deeds recite,
And with great Taſſo celebrate the fight.   22

XXVII.

TO A FRIEND,

OF THE DIFFERENT SUCCESS OF THEIR LOVES.

Thrice happy Pair! of whom we cannot know
Which firſt began to love, or loves moſt now:
Fair courſe of paſſion! where two lovers ſtart,
And run together, heart ſtill yok'd with heart:
Succeſsful Youth! whom Love has taught the way 5
To be victorious in the firſt eſſay.
Sure love's an art beſt practiſed at firſt
And where th' experienced ſtill proſper worſt!
I with a diff'rent fate purſu'd in vain
The haughty Cælia, till my juſt diſdain   10
Of her neglect, above that paſſion borne,
Did pride to pride oppoſe, and ſcorn to ſcorn.
Now ſhe relents; but all too late to move
A heart directed to a nobler love.
The ſcales are turn'd, her kindneſs weighs no more
Now than my vows and ſervice did before.   16
So in ſome well-wrought hangings you may ſee
How Hector leads, and how the Grecians flee:
Here the fierce Mars his courage ſo inſpires,
That with bold hands the Argive fleet he fires: 20

D ij

But there, from heav'n the blue-ey'd virgin * falls,
And frighted Troy retires within her walls:
They that are foremost in that bloody race,
Turn head anon, and give the conqu'rors chase.
So like the chances are of love and war,   25
That they alone in this diftinguifh'd are,
In love the victors from the vanquifh'd fly;
They fly that wound, and they purfue that die.   28

XXVIII.

TO ZELINDA.

FAIREST piece of well-form'd earth!
Urge not thus your haughty birth:
The pow'r which you have o'er us lies
Not in your race, but in your eyes.
" None but a Prince!"—Alas! that voice   5
Confines you to a narrow choice.
Should you no honey vow to tafte,
But what the mafter-bees have plac'd
In compafs of their cells, how fmall
A portion to your fhare would fall?   10
Nor all appear, among thofe few,
Worthy the ftock from whence they grew.
The fap which at the root is bred
In trees, thro' all the boughs is fpread;

              * Minerva.

But virtues which in parents shine, 15
Make not like progress thro' the line.
'Tis not from whom, but where, we live:
The place does oft' those graces give.
Great Julius, on the mountains bred,
A flock perhaps, or herd, had led. 20
He that the world subdu'd *, had been
But the best wrestler on the green.
'Tis art and knowledge which draw forth
The hidden seeds of native worth:
They blow those sparks, and make them rise 25
Into such flames as touch the skies.
To the old heroes hence was giv'n
A pedigree which reach'd to heav'n:
Of mortal seed they were not held,
Which other mortals so excell'd. 30
And beauty, too, in such excess
As your's, Zelinda! claims no less.
Smile but on me, and you shall scorn,
Henceforth, to be of princes born.
I can describe the shady grove 35
Where your lov'd mother slept with Jove,
And yet excuse the faultless dame,
Caught with her spouse's shape and name.
Thy matchless form will credit bring
To all the wonders I shall sing. 40

* Alexander.

D iij

XXIX.

TO MY LADY MORTON,

on new-year's day,

AT THE LOUVRE IN PARIS.

Madam! new years may well expect to find
Welcome from you, to whom they are so kind;
Still as they pass they court and smile on you,
And make your beauty, as themselves, seem new.
To the fair Villars we Dalkeith prefer,   5
And fairest Morton now as much to her:
So like the sun's advance your titles show,
Which as he rises does the warmer grow.
   But thus to style you Fair, your sex's praise,
Gives you but myrtle, who may challenge bays.   10
From armed foes to bring a Royal prize *;
Shews your brave heart victorious as your eyes.
If Judith, marching with the general's head,
Can give us passion when her story's read,
What may the living do, which brought away,   15
Tho' a less bloody, yet a nobler prey;
Who from our flaming Troy, with a bold hand,
Snatch'd her fair charge, the Princess, like a brand?
A brand! preserv'd to warm some prince's heart, 19
And make whole kingdoms take her brother's† part.

---

* Henrietta Maria, youngest daughter to K. Charles I.
† K. Charles II.

So Venus, from prevailing Greeks, did fhrowd
The hope of Rome *, and fav'd him in a cloud.
   This gallant act may cancel all our rage,
Begin a better, and abfolve this age.
Dark fhades become the portrait of our time ;   25
Here weeps Misfortune, and there triumphs Crime!
Let him that draws it hide the reft in night;
This portion only may endure the light,
Where the kind nymph, changing her faultlefs fhape,
Becomes unhandfome, handfomely to 'fcape,   30
When thro' the guards, the river, and the fea,
Faith, Beauty, Wit, and Courage, made their way.
As the brave eagle does with forrow fee
The foreft wafted, and that lofty tree
Which holds her neft about to be o'erthrown,   35
Before the feathers of her young are grown,
She will not leave them, nor fhe cannot flay,
But bears them boldly on her wings away:
So fled the dame, and o'er the ocean bore
Her princely burthen to the Gallic fhore.   40
Born in the ftorms of war, this Royal Fair,
Produc'd like lightning in tempeftuous air,
Tho' now fhe flies her native ifle, (lefs kind,
Lefs fafe for her than either fea or wind!)
Shall, when the bloffom of her beauty's blown,   45
See her great brother on the Britifh throne;
Where Peace fhall fmile, and no difpute arife,
But which rules moft, his fceptre, or her eyes.   48

* Aeneas

XXX.

TO A FAIR LADY,

PLAYING WITH A SNAKE.

STRANGE! that fuch horror and fuch grace
Should dwell together in one place;
A fury's arm, an angel's face!

'Tis innocence and youth which makes
In Chloris' fancy fnch miftakes,
To ftart at love, and play with Snakes.

By this and by her coldnefs barr'd,
Her fervants have a tafk too hard:
The tyrant has a double guard!

Thrice happy Snake! that in her fleeve
May boldly creep; we dare not give
Our thoughts fo unconfin'd a leave.

Contented in that neft of fnow
He lies, as he his blifs did know,
And to the wood no more would go.

Take heed, fair Eve! you do not make
Another tempter of this Snake:
A marble one fo warm'd would fpeak.

XXXI.

A PANEGYRIC TO MY LORD PROTECTOR,

Of the prefent greatnefs, and joint interest,

OF HIS HIGHNESS, AND THIS NATION.

WHILE with a ftrong and yet a gentle hand,
You bridle faction, and our hearts command,
Protect us from ourfelves, and from the foe,
Make us unite, and make us conquer too;

Let partial fpirits ftill aloud complain,   5
Think themfelves injur'd that they cannot reign,
And own no liberty but where they may
Without control upon their fellows prey:

Above the waves as Neptune fhew'd his face,
To chide the winds, and fave the Trojan race,   10
So has your Highnefs, rais'd above the reft,
Storms of ambition toffing us repreft.

Your drooping country, torn with Civil hate,
Reftor'd by you, is made a glorious ftate;
The feat of empire, where the Irifh come,   15
And the unwilling Scots, to fetch their doom.

The fea's our own: and now all nations greet,
With bending fails, each veffel of our fleet.
Your pow'r extends as far as winds can blow,
Or fwelling fails upon the globe may go   20

Heav'n, (that hath plac'd this ifland to give law,
To balance Europe, and her ftates to awe)
In this conjunction doth on Britain fmile,
The greateft leader, and the greateft ifle!

Whether this portion of the world were rent,   25
By the rude ocean, from the continent,
Or thus created, it was fure defign'd
To be the facred refuge of mankind.

Hither th' oppreffed fhall henceforth refort,
Juftice to crave, and fuccour, at your court;   30
And then your Highnefs, not for ours alone,
But for the world's Protector fhall be known.

Fame, fwifter than your winged navy, flies'
'Thro' ev'ry land that near the ocean lies,
Sounding your name. and telling dreadful news   35
To all that piracy and rapine ufe.

With fuch a chief the meaneft nation bleft,
Might hope to lift her head above the reft.
What may be thought impoffible to do
By us embraced by the fea and you?   40

Lords of the world's great wafte, the ocean, we
Whole forefts fend to reign upon the fea,
And ev'ry coaft may trouble or relieve;
But none can vifit us without your leave.

Angels and we have this prerogative, 45
That none can at our happy feats arrive;
While we defcend, at pleafure, to invade
The bad with vengeance, and the good to aid.

Our little world, the image of the great,
Like that, amidft the boundlefs ocean fet, 50
Of her own growth hath all that Nature craves,
And all that's rare, as tribute from the waves.

As Egypt does not on the clouds rely,
But to the Nile owes more than to the fky;
So what our earth and what our heav'n denies 55
Our ever-conftant friend, the fea, fupplies.

The tafte of hot Arabia's fpice we know,
Free from the fcorching fun that makes it grow:
Without the worm, in Perfian filks we fhine;
And, without planting, drink of ev'ry vine. 60

To dig for wealth we weary not our limbs;
Gold, tho' the heavieft metal, hither fwims.
Ours is the harveft where the Indians mow;
We plough the deep, and reap what others fow.

Things of the nobleft kind our own foil breeds; 65
Stout are our men, and warlike are our fteeds.
Rome, tho' her Eagle thro' the world had flown,
Could never make this ifland all her own.

Here the Third Edward, and the Black Prince, too,
France-conqu'ring Henry flourifh'd, and now you; 70
For whom we ftay'd, as did the Grecian ftate,
Till Alexander came to urge their fate.

When for more worlds the Macedonian cry'd,
He wift not Thetis in her lap did hide
Another yet; a world referv'd for you,   75
To make more great than that he did fubdue.

He fafely might old troops to battle lead,
Againft th' unwarlike Perfian and the Mede,
Whofe hafty flight did, from a bloodlefs field,
More fpoils than honour to the victor yield.   80

A race unconquer'd, by their clime made bold,
The Caledonians, arm'd with want and cold,
Have, by a fate indulgent to your fame,
Been from all ages kept for you to tame.

Whom the old Roman wall fo ill confin'd,   85
With a new chain of garrifons you bind:
Here foreign gold no more fhall make them come;
Our Englifh iron holds them faft at home.

They, that henceforth muft be content to know
No warmer region than their hills of fnow,   90
May blame the fun, but muft extol your grace,
Which in our fenate hath allow'd them place.

Preferr'd by conqueſt, happily o'erthrown,
Falling they riſe, to be with us made one.
So kind Dictators made, when they came home, 95
Their vanquiſh'd foes free citizens of Rome.

Like favour find the Iriſh, with like fate
Advanc'd to be a portion of our ſtate ;
While by your valour and your bounteous mind,
Nations, divided by the ſea, are join'd. 100

Holland, to gain your friendſhip, is content
To be our outguard on the Continent :
She from her fellow-provinces would go,
Rather than hazard to have you her foe.

In our late fight, when cannons did diffuſe, 105
Preventing poſts, the terror and the news,
Our neighbour princes trembled at their roar ;
But our conjunction makes them tremble more.

Your never-failing ſword made war to ceaſe,
And now you heal us with the acts of peace ; 110
Our minds with bounty and with awe engage,
Invite affection, and reſtrain our rage.

Leſs pleaſure take brave minds in battles won,
Than in reſtoring ſuch as are undone.
Tigers have courage, and the rugged bear, 115
But man alone can, whom he conquers, ſpare.

To pardon willing, and to punifh loath,
You ftrike with one hand, but you heal with both.
Lifting up all that proftrate lie, you grieve.
You cannot make the dead again to live.   120

When Fate or Error had our age mifled,
And o'er this nation fuch confufion fpread,
The only cure which could from Heav'n come down
Was fo much pow'r and piety in one!

One! whofe extraction from an ancient line   125
Gives hope again that well-born men may fhine.
The meaneft in your nature, mild and good,
The noble reft fecured in your blood.

Oft' have we wonder'd how you hid in peace
A mind proportion'd to fuch things as thefe;   130
How fuch a ruling fp'rit you could reftrain,
And practife firft over yourfelf to reign.

Your private life did a juft pattern give
How fathers, hufbands, pious fons, fhould live.
Born to command, your princely virtues flept,   135
Like humble David's, while the flock he kept:

But when your troubled country call'd you forth,
Your flaming courage and your matchlefs worth,
Dazzling the eyes of all that did pretend,
To fierce contention gave a profp'rous end.   140

Still as you rife, the ftate, exalted too,
Finds no diftemper while 'tis chang'd by you;
Chaug'd like the world's great fcene! when, without
The rifing fun night's vulgar lights deftroys. [noife,

Had you, fome ages paft, this race of glory   145
Run, with amazement we fhould read your ftory;
But living virtue, all achievements paft,
Meets envy ftill to grapple with at laft.

This Cæfar' found; and that ungrateful age,
With lofing him, went back to blood and rage: I5O
Miftaken Brutus thought to break their yoke,
But cut the bond of union with that ftroke.

That fun once fet, a thoufand meaner ftars
Gave a dim light to violence and wars;
To fuch a tempeft as now threatens all,   I55
Did not your mighty arm prevent the fall.

If Rome's great fenate could not wield that fword,
Which of the conquer'd world had made them lord,
What hope had ours, while yet their pow'r was new,
To rule victorious armies, but by you?   I6O

You! that had taught them to fubdue their foes,
Could order teach. and their high fp'rits compofe ;
To ev'ry duty could their minds engage,
Provoke their courage, and command their rage.

                        E ij

So when a lion fhakes his dreadful mane,   163
And angry grows, if he that firft took pain
To tame his youth approach the haughty beaft,
He bends to him, but frights away the reft.

As the vex'd world, to find repofe, at laft
Itfelf into Auguftus' arms did caft;   .   170
So England now does, with like toil oppreft,
Her weary head upon your bofom reft.

Then let the Mufes, with fuch notes as thefe,   .
Inftruct us what belongs unto our peace.
Your battles they hereafter fhall indite, . . .   175
And draw the image of our Mars in fight :

Tell of towns ftorm'd, of armies over-run, ..   .
And mighty kingdoms by your conduct won ;   '
How, while you thunder'd, clouds of duft did choke
Contending troops, and feas lay hid in fmoke. 186

Illuftrious acts high raptures do infufe,
And ev'ry conqueror creates a Mufe.   . /
Here, in low ftrains, your milder deeds we fing;
But there, my Lord! we'll bays and olive bring · .

To crown your head: while you in triumph ride 185
O'er vanquifh'd nations, and the fea befide;   '
While all your neighbour-princes unto you;   ·'
Like Jofeph's fheaves, pay reverence, and bow. 188

XXXII.

TO THE KING,

UPON HIS MAJESTY'S HAPPY RETURN.

The rifing fun complies with our weak fight,
Firft gilds the clouds, then fhows his globe of light,
At fuch a diftance from our eyes, as tho'
He knew what harm his hafty beams would do.
 But your full majefty at once breaks forth   5
In the meridian of your reign. Your worth,
Your youth, and all the fplendour of your ftate,
(Wrapp'd up, till now, in clouds of adverfe fate!)
With fuch a flood of light invade our eyes,
And our fpread hearts with fo great joy furprife, 10
That if your grace incline that we fhould live,
You muft not, Sir! too haftily forgive.
Our guilt preferves us from th' excefs of joy,
Which fcatters fpirits, and would life deftroy.
All are obnoxious! and this faulty land,   15
Like fainting Efther, does before you 'ftand,
Watching your fceptre. The revolted fea
Trembles to think fhe did your foes obey.
 Great Britain, like blind Polypheme, of late,
In a wild rage became the fcorn and hate   20
Of her proud neighbours, who began to think
She with the weight of her own force would fink.

But you are come, and all their hopes are vain;
This Giant Isle has got her eye again.
Now she might spare the ocean, and oppose　　25
Your conduct to the fiercest of her foes.
Naked, the Graces guarded you from all
Dangers abroad, and now your thunder shall.
Princes that saw you diff'rent passions prove,
For now they dread the object of their love,　　30
Nor without envy can behold his height,
Whose conversation was their late delight.
So Semele, contented with the rape
Of Jove, disguised in a mortal shape,
When she beheld his hands with lightning fill'd, 35
And his bright rays, was with amazement kill'd.

　　And tho' it be our sorrow and our crime
To have accepted life so long a time
Without you here, yet does this absence gain
No small advantage to your present reign:　　40
For having view'd the persons and the things,
The councils, state, and strength of Europe's kings,
You know your work; ambition to restrain,
And set them bounds, as Heav'n does to the main.
We have you now with ruling wisdom fraught,　45
Not such as books, but such as practise taught.
So the lost sun, while least by us enjoy'd,
Is the whole night for our concern employ'd:
He ripens spices, fruits, and precious gums,
Which from remotest regions hither comes.　　50

This feat of your's (from th' other world remov'd)
Had Archimedes known, he might have prov'd
His engine's force fix'd here. Your pow'r and skill
Make the world's motion wait upon your will.

Much suff'ring Monarch! the first English-born 55
That has the crown of these three nations worn!
How has your patience, with the barb'rous rage
Of your own soil, contended half an age?
Till (your try'd virtue and your sacred word,
At last preventing your unwilling sword) 60
Armies and fleets which kept you out so long,
Own'd their great Sov'reign, and redress'd his wrong.
When straight the people, by no force compell'd,
Nor longer from their inclination held,
Break forth at once, like powder set on fire, 65
And, with a noble rage, their King require.
So th' injur'd sea, which from her wonted course,
To gain some acres, avarice did force,
If the new banks, neglected once, decay,
No longer will from her old channel stay; 70
Raging, the late-got land she overflows,
And all that's built upon't to ruin goes.

Offenders now, the chiefest, do begin
To strive for grace, and expiate their sin.
All winds blow fair, that did the world embroil; 75
Your vipers treacle yield, and scorpions oil.

If then such praise the Macedonian* got,
For having rudely cut the Gordian knot,

* Alexander.

What glory's due to him that could divide
Such ravell'd int'rests? has the knot unty'd,   80
And without stroke so smooth a passage made,
Where Craft and Malice such impeachments laid?

   But while we praise you, you ascribe it all
To His high hand which threw the untouch'd wall
Of self-demolish'd Jericho so low: 85
His angel 'twas that did before you go,
Tam'd savage hearts, and made affections yield,
Like ears of corn when wind salutes the field.

   Thus, patience-crown'd, like Job's, your trouble ends,
Having your foes to pardon and your friends: 90
For tho' your courage were so firm a rock,
What private virtue could endure the shock?
Like your Great Master, you the storm withstood,
And pity'd those who love with frailty shew'd.

   Rude Indians, tort'ring all the royal race,   95
Him with the throne and dear-bought sceptre grace
That suffers best. What region could be found,
Where your heroic head had not been crown'd?

   The next experience of your mighty mind
Is, how you combat Fortune, now she's kind.   100
And this way, too, you are victorious found;
She flatters with the same success she frown'd.
While to yourself severe, to others kind,
With pow'r unbounded and a will confin'd,
Of this vast empire you possess the care,   105
The softer parts fall to the people's share.

Safety and equal government are things
Which subjects make as happy as their kings.
   Faith, Law, and Piety, (that banish'd train!)
Justice and Truth, with you return again.   110
The City's trade, and country's easy life,
Once more shall flourish without fraud or strife.
Your reign no less assures the ploughman's peace,
Than the warm sun advances his increase;
And does the shepherds as securely keep,   115
From all their fears, as they preserve their sheep.
   But, above all, the Muse-inspired train
Triumph, and raise their drooping heads again:
Kind Heav'n at once, has, in your person sent
Their sacred judge, their guard, and argument.   120

Nec magis expressi vultus per ahenea signa,
Quam per vatis opus mores, animique, virorum
Clarorum apparent * * * *.

                                        Hor.

XXXIII.

TO THE QUEEN,

UPON HER MAJESTY'S BIRTH-DAY,

after her happy recovery from a dangerous sickness.

Farewell the year which threaten'd so
The fairest light the world can show.
Welcome the new! whose ev'ry day,
Restoring what was snatch'd away

By pining ficknefs from the fair,
That matchlefs beauty does repair
So faft, that the approaching fpring,
(Which does to flow'ry meadows bring
What the rude winter from them tore)
Shall give her all fhe had before.

But we recover not fo faft
The fenfe of fuch a danger paft:
We that efteem'd you fent from heav'n,
A pattern to this ifland giv'n,
To fhew us what the blefs'd do there,
And what alive they practis'd here,
When that which we immortal thought,
We faw fo near deftruction brought,
Felt all which you did then endure,
And tremble yet as not fecure:
So tho' the fun victorious be,
And from a dark eclipfe fet free,
The influence, which we fondly fear,
Afflicts our thoughts the following year.

But that which may relieve our care
Is, that you have a help fo near
For all the evil you can prove,
The kindnefs of your Royal love:
He that was never known to mourn,
So many kingdoms from him torn,
His tears referv'd for you, more dear,
More priz'd, than all thofe kingdoms were!

For when no healing art prevail'd,
When cordials and elixirs fail'd,
On your pale cheek he dropp'd the fhow'r
Reviv'd you like a dying flow'r.   36

XXXIV.

TO THE DUCHESS OF ORLEANS,

when fhe was taking leave of

THE COURT AT DOVER.

That fun of beauty did among us rife;
England firft faw the light of your fair eyes:
In Englifh, too, your early wit was fhown;
Favour that language, which was then your own,
When, tho' a child, thro' guards you made you way:
What fleet or army could an angel ftay?   6
Thrice happy Britain! if fhe could retain
Whom fhe firft bred within her ambient main.
Our late burnt London, in apparel new,
Shook off her afhes to have treated you: 10.
But we muft fee our glory fnatch'd away,
And with warm tears increafe the guilty fea:
No wind can favour us; howe'er it blows,
We muft be wreck'd, and our dear treafure lofe!
Sighs will not let us half our forrows tell——
Fair, lovely, great, and beft of nymphs, farewell' 16

XXXV.

TO A LADY,

*From whom he received the copy of the poem entitled, Of
a Tree cut in Paper, which for many years had been loft.*

Nothing lies hid from radiant eyes;
All they fubdue become their fpies.
Secrets, as choiceft jewels, are
Prefented to oblige the fair:
No wonder, then, that a loft thought   5
Should there be found where fouls are caught.
   The picture of fair Venus (that
For which men fay the goddefs fat)
Was loft, till Lely from your look
Again that glorious image took.   10
   If Virtue's felf were loft, we might
From your fair mind new copies write.
All things but one you can reftore;
The heart you get returns no more.   14

XXXVI.

TO MR. KILLEGREW,

*Upon his altering his play, Pandora, from a tragedy into
a comedy, becaufe not approved on the ftage.*

Sir! you fhould rather teach our age the way
Of judging well, than thus have chang'd your play.
   5

You had oblig'd us by employing wit
Not to reform Pandora, but the Pit :
For as the nightingale, without the throng   5
Of other birds, alone attends her song,
While the loud daw, his throat difplaying, draws
The whole affembly of his fellow-daws ;
So muft the writer whofe productions fhould
Take with the vulgar be of vulgar mould ;   10
Whilft nobler fancies make a flight too high
For common view, and leffen as they fly.   12

XXXVII.

TO A FRIEND OF THE AUTHOR,

A PERSON OF HONOUR,

*Who lately writ a religious book, entitled, Hiftorical Appli-
cations, and occafional Meditations, upon feveral fubjects.*

BOLD is the man that dares engage
For piety in fuch an age !
Who can prefume to find a guard
From fcorn, when Heav'n's fo little fpar'd ?
Divines are pardon'd ; they defend   5
Altars on which their lives depend ;
But the profane impatient are,
When nobler pens make this their care ;
For why fhould thefe let in a beam
Of divine light to trouble them,   10
   Volume II.   F

And call in doubt their pleafing thought,
That none believes what we are taught?
High birth and fortune warrant give
That fuch men write what they believe;
And, feeling firft what they indite,   15
New credit give to ancient light.
Amongft thefe few, our author brings
His well-known pedigree from kings.
This book, the image of his mind,
Will make his name not hard to find: 20
I wifh the throng of great and good
Made it lefs ens'ly underftood!   22

XXXVIII.

TO A PERSON OF HONOUR,

Upon his incomparable, incomprehenfible poem, entitled, The
    Britifh Princes.

Sir! you've oblig'd the Britifh nation more
Than all their bards could ever do before,
And at your own charge monnments as hard
As brafs or marble to your fame have rear'd:
For as all warlike nations take delight   5
To hear how their brave anceftors could fight,
You have advanc'd to wonder their renown,
And no lefs virtuoufly improv'd your own;

That 'twill be doubtful whether you do write
Or they have acted at a nobler height.   10
You of your ancient princes have retriev'd
More than the ages knew in which they liv'd;
Explain'd their customs and their rights a-new,
Better than all their Druids ever knew;
Unriddled those dark oracles as well   15
As those that made them could themselves foretell.
For as the Britons long have hop'd, in vain,
Arthur would come to govern them again,
You have fulfill'd that prophesy alone,
And in your poem plac'd him on his throne.   20
Such magic pow'r has your prodigious pen
To raise the dead, and give new life to men,
Make rival princes meet in arms, and love
Whom distant ages did so far remove:
For as eternity has neither past   25
Nor future, authors say, nor first nor last,
But is all instant, your eternal Muse
All ages can to any one reduce.
Then why should you, whose miracles of art
Can life at pleasure to the dead impart,   30
Trouble in vain your better-busied head,
T' observe what times they liv'd in or were dead?
For since you have such arbitrary pow'r,
It were defect in judgment to go low'r,
Or stoop to things so pitifully lewd,   35
As use to take the vulgar latitude :

F ij

For no man's fit to read what you have writ,
That holds not some proportion with your wit:
As light can no way but by light appear,
He muſt bring ſenſe that underſtands it here.

XXXIX.

TO CHLORIS.

Chloris! what's eminent, we know
Muſt for ſome cauſe be valu'd ſo:
Things without uſe, tho' they be good,
Are not by us ſo underſtood.
The early roſe, made to diſplay
Her bluſhes to the youthful May,
Doth yield her ſweets, ſince he is fair,
And courts her with a gentle air.
Our ſtars do ſhew their excellence
Not by their light, but influence:
When brighter comets, ſince ſtill known,
Fatal to all, are lik'd by none.
So your admired beauty ſtill
Is, by effects, made good or ill.

XL.

TO THE KING.

Great Sir! diſdain not in this piece to ſtand
Supreme commander both of ſea and land.

Thofe which inhabit the celeftial bow'r,
Painters exprefs with emblems of their pow'r;
His club Alcides, Phœbus has his bow,   5
Jove has his thunder, and your navy you.

But your great providence no colours here
Can reprefent, nor pencil draw that care
Which keeps you waking to fecure our peace,
The nation's glóry, and our trade's increafe :   10
You for thefe ends whole days in council fit,
And the diverfions of your youth forget.

Small were the worth of valour and of force,
If your high wifdom govern'd not their courfe :
You as the foul, as the firft mover you,   15
Vigour and life on ev'ry part beftow :
How to build fhips, and dreadful ord'nance caft,
Inftruct the artifts, and reward their hafte.

So Jove himfelf, when Typhon heav'n does brave,
Defcends to vifit Vulcan's fmoky cave,   20
Teaching the brawny Cyclops how to frame
His thunder, mix'd with terror, wrath, and flame.
Had the old Greeks difcover'd your abode,
Crete had not been the cradle of their god :
On that fmall ifland they had look'd with fcorn,
And in Great Britain thought the Thund'rer born: 26

F iij

XLI.

TO THE DUCHESS,

when he prefented

THIS BOOK TO HER ROYAL HIGHNESS.

Madam! I here prefent you with the rage,
And with the beauties of a former age,
Wifhing you may with as great pleafure view
This, as we take in gazing upon you.
'Thus we writ then: your brighter eyes infpire   5
A nobler flame, and raife our genius high'r.
While we your wit and early knowledge fear,
'To our productions we become fevere :
Your matchlefs beauty gives our fancy wing,
Your judgment makes us careful how we fing.   10
Lines not compos'd, as heretofore, in hafte,
Polifh'd like marble, fhall like marble laft,
And make you thro' as many ages fhine,
As Taffo has the heroes of your line.

Tho' other names our wary writers ufe,   15
You are the fubject of the Britifh Mufe :
Dilating mifchief to yourfelf unknown,
Men write, and die of wounds they dare not own.
So the bright fun burns all our grafs away,
While it means nothing but to give us day.   20

SONGS.

I.

SONG.

Stay, Phœbus! ftay;
The world to which you fly fo faft,
Conveying day
From us to them, can pay your hafte
With no fuch objeĉt, nor falute your rife   5
With no fuch wonder as De Mornay's eyes.

Well does this prove
The error of thofe antique books
Which made you move
About the world : her charming looks   10
Would fix your beams, and make it ever day,
Did not t he rolling earth fnatch her away.   12

II.

SONG.

Say, lovely Dream ! where couldft thou find
Shades to counterfeit that face?
Colours of this glorious kind
Come not from any mortal place.

In heav'n itfelf thou fure wert dreft   i
With that angel-like difguife:
Thus deluded am I bleft,
And fee my joy with clofed eyes.

But, ah! this image is too kind
To be other than a Dream: 10
Cruel Sachariffa's mind
Never put on that fweet extreme!

Fair Dream! if thou intend'ft me grace,
Change that heav'nly face of thine;
Paint defpis'd love in thy face,   15
And make it to appear like mine.

Pale, wan, and meagre, let it look,
With a pity-moving fhape,
Such as wander by the brook
Of Lethe, or from graves'efcapes.   20

Then to that matchlefs nymph appear,
In whofe fhape thou fhineft fo;
Softly in her fleeping ear,
With humble words, exprefs my woe.

Perhaps from greatnefs, ftate, and pride,   25
Thus furprifed fhe may fall:
Sleep does difproportion hide,
And, death refembling, equals all.   28

III.

SONG.

PEACE, babbling Mufe!
I dare not fing what you indite;
Her eyes refufe
To read the paffion which they write:
She ftrikes my lute, but if it found,
Threatens to hurl it on the ground:
And I no lefs her anger dread,
Than the poor wretch that feigns him dead,
While fome fierce lion does embrace
His breathlefs corpfe, and lick his face :
Wrapp'd up in filent fear he lies,
Torn all in pieces if he cries.

IV.

SONG.

I.

CHLORIS! farewell; I now muft go;
For if with thee I longer ftay,
Thy eyes prevail upon me fo,
I fhall prove blind, and lofe my way.
II.
Fame of thy beauty and thy youth,
Among the reft, me hither brought :

Finding this fame fall fhort of truth,
Made me ftay longer than I thought.

III.

For I'm engag'd by word and oath,
A fervant to another's will;
Yet for thy love I'd forfeit both,
Could I be fure to keep it ftill.

IV.

But what affurance can I take;
When thou, foreknowing this abufe,
For fome more worthy lover's fake;
May'ft leave me with fo juft excufe?

V.

For thou may'ft fay, 'twas not thy fault
That thou didft thus inconftant prove,
Being by my example taught
To break thy oath to mend thy love.

VI.

No, Chloris! no: I will return,
And raife thy ftory to that height,
That ftrangers fhall at diftance burn,
And fhe diftruft me reprobate.

VII.

Then fhall my love this doubt difplace,
And gain fuch truft, that I may come
And banquet fometimes on thy face,
But make my conftant meals at home.

V.

SONG. TO FLAVIA.

I.

'Tis not your beauty can engage
My wary heart;
The ſun, in all his pride and rage,
Has not that art;
And yet he ſhines as bright as you,
If brightneſs could our ſouls ſubdue.

II.

'Tis not the pretty things you ſay,
Nor thoſe you write,
Which can make Thyrſis' heart your prey:
For that delight,
The graces of a well-taught mind
In ſome of our own ſex we find.

III.

No, Flavia! 'tis your love I fear;
Love's ſureſt darts,
Thoſe which ſo ſeldom fail him, are
Headed with hearts:
Their very ſhadows make us yield;
Diſſemble well, and win the field.

VI.

SONG.

Behold the brand of Beauty toſt!
See how the motion does dilate the flame!

Delighted Love his fpoils does boaft,
And triumph in this game.
Fire, to no place confin'd,
Is both our wonder and our fear,
Moving the mind,
As lightning hurled thro' the air.

High heav'n the glory does increafe
Of all her fhining lamps this artful way;
The fun in figures, fuch as thefe,
Joys with the moon to play:
To the fweet ftrains they advance,
Which do refult from their own fpheres,
As this nymph's dance
Moves with the numbers which fhe hears.

VII.

SONG.

WHILE I liften to thy voice,
Chloris! I feel my life decay;
That pow'rful noife
Calls my fleeting foul away.
Oh! fupprefs that magic found,
Which deftroys without a wound.

Peace, Chloris! peace! or finging die,
That together you and I
2.

To heav'n may go;
For all we know   10
Of what the bleſſed do above,
Is that they ſing, and that they love.   12

VIII.

SONG.

Go, lovely Roſe!
Tell her that waſtes her time and me,
That now ſhe knows,
When I reſemble her to thee,
How ſweet and fair ſhe ſeems to be.   5

Tell her that's young,
And ſhuns to have her graces ſpy'd,
That hadſt thou ſprung
In deſerts, where no men abide,
Thou muſt have uncommended dy'd.   10

Small is the worth
Of beauty from the light retir'd :
Bid her come forth,
Suffer herſelf to be deſir'd,
And not bluſh ſo to be admir'd.   15

Then die ! that she
The common fate of all things rare
May read in thee,
How small a part of time they share
That are so wondrous sweet and fair!

IX.

SUNG BY

MRS. KNIGHT, TO HER MAJESTY,

ON HER BIRTH-DAY.

THIS happy day two lights are seen,
A glorious Saint, a matchless Queen;
Both nam'd alike, both crown'd appear,
The saint above, th' Infanta here.
May all those years which Catharine
The Martyr did for heav'n resign,
Be added to the line
Of your blest life among us here!
For all the pains that she did feel,
And all the torments of her wheel,
May you as many pleasures share!
May Heav'n itself content
With Catharine the Saint!
Without appearing old,
An hundred times may you,
With eyes as bright as now,
This welcome day behold!

PROLOGUES AND EPILOGUES.

I.

PROLOGUE FOR THE LADY-ACTORS:

SPOKEN BEFORE K. CHARLES II.

Amaze us not with that majeftic frown,
But lay afide the greatnefs of your crown!
And for that look which does your people awe,
When in your throne and robes you give them law,
Lay it by here, and give a gentler fmile,   5
Such as we fee great Jove's in picture, while
He liftens to Apollo's charming lyre,
Or judges of the fongs he does infpire.
Comedians on the ftage fhew all their fkill,
And after do as Love and Fortune will.   10
We are lefs careful, hid in this difguife;
In our own clothes more ferious and more wife.
Modeft at home, upon the ftage more bold,
We feem warm lovers, tho' our breafts be cold:
A fault committed here deferves no fcorn,
If we act well the parts to which we're born.   16

G ij

II.

PROLOGUE

TO THE MAID'S TRAGEDY.

Scarce fhould we have the boldnefs to pretend
So long-renown'd a tragedy to mend,
Had not already fome deferv'd your praife
With like attempt. Of all our elder plays
This and Philafter have the loudeft fame :   5
Great are their faults, and glorious is their flame.
In both our Englifh genius is exprefs'd;
Lofty and bold, but negligently drefs'd:
   Above our neighbours our conceptions are;
But faultlefs writing is th'effect of care.   10
Our lines reform'd, and not compos'd in hafte,
Polifh'd like marble, would like marble laft:
But as the prefent, fo the laft age writ;
In both we find like negligence and wit.
Were we but lefs indulgent to our faults,   15
And patience had to cultivate our thoughts,
Our Mufe would flourifh, and a nobler rage
Would honour this than did the Grecian ftage.
   Thus fays our Author, not content to fee
That others write as carelefsly as he;   20
Tho' he pretends not to make things complete,
Yet, to pleafe you, he'd have the poets fweat.
   In this old play, what's new we have expreft
In rhyming verfe, diftinguifh'd from the reft;

That as the Rhone its hafty way does make 25
(Not mingling waters) thro' Geneva's lake,
So having here the diff'rent ftyles in view,
You may compare the former with the new.

    If we lefs rudely fhall the knot unty,
Soften the rigour of the tragedy, 30
And yet preferve each perfon's character,
Then to the other this you may prefer.
'Tis left to you : the Boxes and the Pit
Are fov'reign judges of this fort of wit.
In other things the knowing artift may 35
Judge better than the people ; but a play,
(Made for delight, and for no other ufe)
If you approve it not, has no excufe. 38

III.

EPILOGUE

TO THE MAID'S TRAGEDY. SPOKEN BY THE KING.

THE fierce Melantius was content, you fee,
The King fhould live ; be not more fierce than he :
Too long indulgent to fo rude a time,
When love was held fo capital a crime,
That a crown'd head could no compaffion find, 5
But dy'd——becaufe the killer had been kind!
Nor is 't lefs ftrange fuch mighty wits as thofe
Should ufe a ftyle in tragedy like profe.

Well-founding verse, where princes tread the stage,
Should speak their virtue, or describe their rage.   10
By the loud trumpet, which our courage aids,
We learn that found, as well as fenfe, perfuades:
And verfes are the potent charms we ufe,
Heroic thoughts and virtue to infufe.

    When next we act this tragedy again,   15
Unlefs you like the change, we fhall be flain.
The innocent Afpafia's life or death;
Amintor's too, depends upon your breath.
Excefs of love was heretofore the caufe;
Now if we die 'tis want of your applaufe.   20

IV.

EPILOGUE

TO THE MAID'S TRAGEDY.

*Defigned upon the firft alteration of the play, when the
King only was left alive.*

Aspasia bleeding on the ftage does ly,
To fhew you ftill 'tis the Maid's Tragedy.
The fierce Melantius was content, you fee,
The King fhould live: be not more fierce than he:
Too long indulgent to fo rude a time,   5
When love was held fo capital a crime,
That a crown'd head could no compaffion find,
But dy'd——becaufe the killer had been kind!

This better-natur'd Poet had repriev'd
Gentle Amintor too, had he believ'd   10
The fairer fex his pardon could approve,
Who to ambition facrific'd his love.
Afpafia he has fpar'd; but for her wound
(Neglected love!) there could no falve be found.

When next we act this tragedy again,   15
Unlefs you like the change, I muft be flain.
Excefs of love was heretofore the caufe;
Now if I die 'tis want of your applaufe.   18

I. *Under a lady's picture.*

Such Helen was! and who can blame the boy *
That in so bright a flame consum'd his Troy?
But had like virtue shin'd in that fair Greek,
The am'rous shepherd had not dar'd to seek
Or hope for pity, but with silent moan,
And better fate, had perished alone.   6

II. *Of a lady who writ in praise of Mira.*

While she pretends to make the graces known
Of matchless Mira, she reveals her own :
And when she would another's praise indite,
Is by her glass instructed how to write.   4

III. *To one married to an old man.*

Since thou wouldst needs (bewitch'd with some ill
Be bury'd in those monumental arms,   [charms!)
All we can wish is, may that earth lie light
Upon thy tender limbs! and so good night.   4

IV. *An epigram on a painted lady with ill teeth.*

Were men so dull they could not see
That Lyce painted; should they flee,

* Paris.

Like simple birds, into a net'
So grosly woven and ill set,
Her own teeth would undo the knot,   5
And let all go that she had got.
Those teeth fair Lyce must not show
If she would bite : her lovers, tho'
Like birds they stoop at seeming grapes,
Are disabus'd when first she gapes :   10
The rotten bones discover'd there,
Shew 'tis a painted sepulchre.   12

V. *Epigram upon the golden medal.*

Our guard upon the royal side!
On the reverse our beauty's pride!
Here we discern the frown and smile,
The force and glory of our isle.
In the rich medal, both so like   5
Immortals stand, it seems antique;
Carv'd by some master, when the bold
Greeks made their Jove descend in gold,
And Danae wond'ring at that show'r,
Which, falling, storm'd her brazen tow'r;   10
Britannia there, the fort in vain
Had batter'd been with golden rain:
Thunder itself had fail'd to pass:
Virtue's a stronger guard than brass.   14

VI. *Written on a card that her Majesty* * *tore at Ombre.*

THE cards you tear in value rife;
So do the wounded by your eyes.
Who to celeftial things afpire,
Are by that paffion rais'd the higher.   4

VII. *To Mr. Granville, (now Lord Lanfdown) on his
verfes to K. James II.*

AN early plant ! which fuch a bloffom bears,
And fhews a genius fo beyond his years :
A judgment ! that could make fo fair a choice ;
So high a fubject to employ his voice :
Still as it grows, how fweetly will he fing
The growing greatnefs of our matchlefs King !   6

VIII. *Long and fhort life.*

CIRCLES are prais'd, not that abound
In largenefs, but th' exactly round :
So life we praife that does excel
Not in much time, but acting well.   4

IX. *Tranflated out of Spanifh.*

THO' we may feem importunate,
While your compaffion we implore,
They whom you make too fortunate,
May with prefumption vex you more.   4

* Q. Catharine.

X. *Translated out of French.*

FADE, Flowers! fade, Nature will have it fo;
'Tis but what we muft in our autumn do!
And as your leaves lie quiet on the ground,
The lofs alone by thofe that lov'd them found;   4
So in the grave fhall we as quiet ly,
Mifs'd by fome few that lov'd our company:
But fome fo like to thorns and nettles live,
That none for them can, when they perifh, grieve. 8

XI. *Some verfes of an imperfect copy, defigned for a friend, on his tranflation of Ovid's Fafti.*

ROME's holy-days you tell, as if a gueft
With the old Romans you were wont to feaft.
Numa's religion, by themfelves believ'd,
Excels the true, only in fhew receiv'd.
They made the nations round about them bow,   5
With their Dictators taken from the plow:
Such pow'r has juftice, faith, and honefty!
The world was conquer'd by morality.
Seeming devotion does but gild a knave,
That's neither faithful, honeft, juft, nor brave;   10
But where religion does with virtue join,
It makes a hero like an angel fhine.   12

* * * * * * * * * * * * * *

XII. *On the statue of King Charles I. at Charing-cross, in the year* 1674.

THAT the First Charles does here in triumph ride,
See his son reign'd where he a martyr dy'd,
And people pay that rev'rence as they pass,
(Which then he wanted!) to the sacred brass,
Is not th' effect of gratitude alone,   5
To which we owe the statue and the stone;
But Heav'n this lasting monument has wrought,
That mortals may eternally be taught
Rebellion, tho' successful, is but vain,
And kings so kill'd rise conquerors again.   10
This truth the royal image does proclaim,
Loud as the trumpet of surviving Fame.   12

XIII. *Pride.*

NOT the brave Macedonian youth * alone,
But base Caligula, when on the throne,
Boundless in pow'r, would make himself a god,
As if the world depended on his nod.
The Syrian King † to beasts was headlong thrown, 5
Ere to himself he could be mortal known.
The meanest wretch, if Heav'n should give him line,
Would never stop till he were thought divine.
All might within discern the serpent's pride,
If from ourselves nothing ourselves did hide.   10

* Alexander.   † Nebuchadnezzar.

Let the proud peacock his gay feathers spread,
And woo the female to his painted bed;
Let winds and seas together rage and swell;
This Nature teaches, and becomes them well.
" Pride was not made for men * :" a conscious sense
Of guilt, and folly, and their consequence,   16
Destroys the claim, and to beholders tells,
Here nothing but the shape of Manhood dwells.   18

XIV. *Epitaph on Sir George Speke.*

UNDER this stone lies virtue, youth,
Unblemish'd probity, and truth :
Just unto all relations known,
A worthy patriot, pious son;
Whom neighb'ring towns so often sent,   5
To give their sense in parliament;
With lives and fortunes trusting one
Who so discreetly us'd his own.
Sober he was, wise, temperate,
Contented with an old estate,   10
Which no foul av'rice did increase,
Nor wanton luxury make less.
While yet but young, his father dy'd,
And left him to an happy guide :
Not Lemuel's mother with more care   15
Did counsel or instruct her heir,

* Eccluf. chap. x. ver. 18.

Or teach with more fuccefs her fon
The vices of the time to fhun.
An heirefs fhe; while yet alive,
All that was her's to him did give;   20
And he juft gratitude did fhow
To one that had oblig'd him fo:
Nothing too much for her he thought,
By whom he was fo bred and taught.
So (early made that path to tread,   25
Which did his youth to honour lead)
His fhort life did a pattern give
How neighbours, hufbands, friends, fhould live.
    The virtues of a private life
Exceed the glorious noife and ftrife   30
Of battles won: in thofe we find
The folid int'reft of mankind.
    Approv'd by all, and lov'd fo well,
Tho' young, like fruit that's ripe he fell.   34

XV. *Epitaph on Colonel Charles Cavendiſh.*

HERE lies Charles Ca'ndifh: let the marble ftone,
That hides his afhes, make his virtue known.
Beauty and valour did his fhort life grace,
The grief and glory of his noble race!
Early abroad he did the world furvey,   5
As if he knew he had not long to ftay:
Saw what great Alexander in the Eaft
And mighty Julius conquer'd in the Weft:

Then with a mind as great as theirs he came
To find at home occasion for his fame;   10
Where dark confusion did the nations hide,
And where the juster was the weaker side.
Two loyal brothers took their Sov'reign's part,
Employ'd their wealth, their courage, and their art:
The elder * did whole regiments afford;   15
The younger brought his conduct and his sword.
Born to command, a leader he begun,
And on the rebels lasting honour won.
The horse instructed by their gen'ral's worth,
Still made the King victorious in the North.   20
Where Ca'ndish fought the Royalists prevail'd;
Neither his courage nor his judgment fail'd.
The current of his vict'ries found no stop,
Till Cromwell came, his party's chiefest prop.
Equal success had set these champions high,   25
And both resolv'd to conquer or to die.
Virtue with rage, fury with valour strove;
But that must fall which is decreed above!
Cromwell with odds of number and of Fate,
Remov'd this bulwark of the church and state;   30
Which the sad issue of the war declar'd,
And made his task to ruin both less hard.
So when the bank, neglected, is o'erthrown,
The boundless torrent does the country drown.

* William Earl of Devonshire.

'Thus fell the young, the lovely, and the brave;
Strew bays and flowers on his honour'd grave!   36

XVI. *Epitaph on the Lady Sedley.*

HERE lies the learned Savil's heir,
So early wife, and lasting fair!
That none, except her years they told,
Thought her a child, or thought her old.
All that her father knew or got,   5
His art, his wealth, fell to her lot;
And she so well improv'd that flock,
Both of his knowledge and his flock,
That Wit and Fortune, reconcil'd
In her, upon each other fmil'd.   10
While she, to ev'ry well-taught mind,
Was so propitiously inclin'd,
And gave such title to her flore,
That none but th' ignorant were poor.
The Mufes daily found fupplies,   15
Both from her hands and from her eyes;
Her bounty did at once engage,
And matchlefs beauty warm their rage;
Such was this dame in calmer days,
Her nation's ornament and praife!   20
But when a ftorm difturb'd our reft,
The port and refuge of th' oppreft.
This made her fortune underftood,
And look'd on as fome public good.

So that (her perſon and her ſtate, 25
Exempted from the common fate)
In all our Civil fury ſhe
Stood, like a ſacred temple, free.
May here her monument ſtand ſo,
To credit this rude age! and ſhow 30
To future times, that even we
Some patterns did of virtue ſee;
And one ſublime example had
Of good among ſo many bad. 34

XVII. *Epitaph to be written under the Latin inſcription
upon the tomb of the only ſon of the Lord Andover.*

'Tis fit the Engliſh reader ſhould be told,
In our own language, what this tomb does hold.
'Tis not a noble corpſe alone does lie
Under this ſtone, but a whole family.
His parents' pious care, their name their joy, 5
And all their hope, lies buried with this boy:
This lovely Youth! for whom we all made moan,
That knew his worth, as he had been our own.
    Had there been ſpace and years enough allow'd,
His courage, wit, and breeding, to have ſhow'd, 10
We had not found, in all the num'rous roll
Of his fam'd anceſtors, a greater ſoul:
His early virtues to that ancient ſtock
Gave as much honour as from thence he took.

Like buds appearing ere the frosts are past;   15
To become man he made such fatal haste,
And to perfection labour'd so to climb,
Preventing slow experience and time,
That 'tis no wonder Death our hopes beguil'd.
He's seldom old that will not be a child.   20

XVIII. *Epitaph unfinished.*

GREAT Soul! for whom Death will no longer stay,
But sends in haste to snatch our bliss away.
O cruel Death! to those you take more kind
Than to the wretched mortals left behind!   4
. Here beauty, youth, and noble virtue, shin'd,
Free from the clouds of pride that shade the mind.
Inspired verse may on this marble live,
But can no honour to thy ashes give———   8

DIVINE POEMS.

OF DIVINE LOVE.

A POEM. IN SIX CANTOS.

Floriferis ut apes in faltibus omnia libanr ;
Sic nos Scripturae depafcimur aurea dicta ;
Aurea! perpetua femper dignillima vita!
Nam divinus amor cum caepit vociferari,
Diffugiunt animi torrores.   Lucretius, lib. iii,

Exul eram, requiefque mihi, non fama, petita eft,
Mens intenta fuis ne foret ufque malis :
Namque ubi mota calent facra mea pectora Mufa,.
Altior humano fpiritus ille malo eft.
                                    Ovid. de Trift. lib. iv. el. i.

The Arguments.

I. ASSERTING the authority of the Scripture, in which this love is revealed.

II. The preference and love of God to man in the creation.

III. The fame love more amply declared in our redemption.

IV. How neceffary this love is to reform mankind, and how excellent in itfelf.

V. Shewing how happy the world would be, if this love were univerfally embraced.

VI. Of preferving this love in our memory, and how ufeful the contemplation thereof is.

CANTO I.

THE Grecian Mufe has all their gods furviv'd,
Nor Jove at us nor Phœbus is arriv'd ;
Frail deities! which firft the poets made,
And then invok'd, to give their fancies aid :
Yet if they ftill divert us with their rage,   5
What may be hop'd for in a better age,

When not from Helicon's imagin'd fpring,
But Sacred Writ, we borrow what we fing?
This with the fabric of the world begun,
Elder than light, and fhall outlaft the fun.   10
Before this oracle, like Dagon, all
The falfe pretenders, Delphos, Ammon, fall: —
Long fince defpis'd and filent, they afford
Honour and triumph to th' eternal Word.

As late philofophy our globe has grac'd,   15
And rolling earth among the planets plac'd,
So has this Book entitled us to heav'n,
And rules to guide us to that manfion giv'n:
Tells the conditions how our peace was made,
And is our pledge for the great Author's aid.   20
His pow'r in Nature's ample book we find,
But the lefs volume does exprefs his mind.

This light unknown, bold Epicurus taught
That his bleft gods vouchfafe us not a thought,
But unconcern'd let all below them flide,   25
As fortune does, or human wifdom, guide.
Religion thus remov'd, the facred yoke,
And band of all fociety, is broke.
What ufe of oaths, of promife, or of teft,
Where men regard no God but intereft?   30
What endlefs war would jealous nations tear,
If none above did witnefs what they fwear? ·
Sad fate of unbelievers, and yet juft,
Among themfelves to find fo little truft!

Were Scripture filent; Nature would proclaim,　35
Without a God, our falfehood and our fhame.
To know our thoughts the object of his eyes,
Is the firft ftep tow'rds being good or wife;
For tho' with judgment we on things reflect,
Our will determines, not our intellect.　40
Slaves to their paffion, reafon men employ
Only to compafs what they would enjoy.
His fear to guard us from ourfelves we need,
And Sacred Writ our reafon does exceed:
For tho' heav'n fhews the glory of the Lord,　45
Yet fomething fhines more glorious in his Word:
His mercy this, (which all his work excels!)
His tender kindnefs and compaffion tells:
While we inform'd by that celeftial Book,
Into the bowels of our Maker look.　50
Love there reveal'd, (which never fhall have end,
Nor had beginning) fhall our fong commend;
Defcribe itfelf, and warm us with that flame
Which firft from Heav'n, to make us happy, came.　54

CANTO II.

The fear of hell, or aiming to be bleft,
Savours too much of private intereft:
This mov'd not Mofes, nor the zealous Paul,
Who for their friends abandon'd foul and all:
A greater yet from heav'n to hell defcends,　5
To fave and make his enemies his friends.

What line of praife can fathom fuch a love,
Which reach'd the loweft bottom from above?
The royal prophet *, that extended grace
From heav'n to earth, meafur'd but half that fpace. 10
The law was regnant, and confin'd his thought;
Hell was not conquer'd when that poet wrote:
Heav'n was fcarce heard of until He came down,
To make the region where love triumphs known.

 That early love of creatures yet unmade,   15
To frame the world th' ALmighty did perfuade;
For love it was that firft created light,
Mov'd on the waters, chas'd away the night
From the rude Chaos, and beftow'd new grace
On things difpos'd of to their proper place: 20
Some to reft here, and fome to fhine above;
Earth, fea, and heav'n, were all th' effects of love.
And love would be return'd: but there was none
That to themfelves or others yet were known:
The world a palace was without a gueft,   25
Till one appears that muft excel the reft:
One! like the Author, whofe capacious mind
Might, by the glorious work, the Maker find;
Might meafure heav'n, and give each ftar a name;
With art and courage the rough ocean tame;   30
Over the globe with fwelling fails might go,
And that 'tis round by his experience know;
Make ftrongeft beafts obedient to his will,
 And ferve his ufe the fertile earth to till.

     * David.

When by his Word God had accomplifh'd all,   35
Man to create he did a council call;
Employ'd his hand, to give the duft he took
A graceful figure and majeftic look;
With his own breath convey'd into his breaft
Life, and a foul fit to command the reft;   40
Worthy alone to celebrate his name
For fuch a gift, and tell from whence it came.
Birds fing his praifes in a wilder note,
But not with lafting numbers and with thought,
Man's great prerogative! but above all   45
His grace abounds in his new fav'rite's fall.

   If he create, it is a world he makes;
If he be angry, the creation fhakes :
From his juft wrath our guilty parents fled;
He curs'd the earth, but bruis'd the ferpent's head. 50
Amidft the ftorm his bounty did exceed,
In the rich promife of the Virgin's feed :
Tho' juftice death, as fatisfaction, craves,
Love finds a way to pluck us from our graves.   54

CANTO III.

Nor willing terror fhould his image move;
He gives a pattern of eternal love ;
His Son defcends to treat a peace with thofe
Which were, and muft have ever been, his foes.
Poor he became, and left his glorious feat   5
To make us humble, and to make us great :

His bus'nefs here was happinefs to give
To thofe whofe malice could not let him live.

    Legions of angels, which he might have us'd,
(For us refolv'd to perifh) he refus'd :   10
While they ftood ready to prevent his lofs,
Love took him up, and nail'd him to the crofs.
Immortal love! which in his bowels reign'd,
That we might be by fuch great love conftrain'd
To make return of love. Upon this pole   15
Our duty does, and our religion, roll.
To love is to believe, to hope, to know;
'Tis an effay, a tafte of heav'n below!

    He to proud potentates would not be known;
Of thofe that lov'd him he was hid from none.   20
Till love appear we live in anxious doubt;
But fmoke will vanifh when that flame breaks out :
This is the fire that would confume our drofs,
Refine, and make us richer by the lofs.

    Could we forbear difpute, and practife love,   25
We fhould agree as angels do above.
Where love prefides, not vice alone does find
No entrance there, but virtues ftay behind :
Both faith, and hope, and all the meaner train
Of mortal virtues, at the door remain.   30
Love only enters as a native there,
For, born in heav'n, it does but fojourn here.

    He that alone would wife and mighty be,
Commands that others love as well as he.

    3

Love as he lov'd!—How can we foar fo high ?— 35
He can add wings when he commands to fly.
Nor fhould we be with this command difmay'd;
He that examples gives will give his aid :
For he took flefh, that where his precepts fail,
His practife, as a pattern, may prevail.   40
His love at once, and dread, inftruct our thought;
As man he fuffer'd, and as God he taught.
Will for the deed he takes : we may with eafe
Obedient be, for if we love we pleafe.
Weak tho' we are, to love is no hard tafk,   45
And love for love is all that Heav'n does afk.
Love! that would all men juft and temp'rate make,
Kind to themfelves and others for his fake.
    'Tis with our minds as with a fertile ground,
Wanting this love they muft with weeds abound, 50
(Unruly paffions) whofe effects are worfe
Than thorns and thiftles fpringing from the curfe, 52

CANTO IV.

To glory man, or mifery, is born,
Of his proud foe the envy, or the fcorn :
Wretched he is, or happy, in extreme;
Bafe in himfelf, but great in Heav'n's efteem :
With love, of all created things the beft ;   5
Without it, more pernicious than the reft;
For greedy wolves unguarded fheep devour
But while their hunger lafts, and then give o'er :

Man's boundlefs avarice his wants exceeds,
And on his neighbours round about him feeds.   10
  His pride and vain ambition are fo vaft,
That, deluge-like, they lay whole nations wafte.
Debauches and excefs (tho' with lefs noife)
As great a portion of mankind deftroys.
The beafts and monfters Hercules oppreft,   15
Might in that age fome provinces infeft:
Thefe more deftructive monfters are the bane
Of ev'ry age, and in all nations reign;
But foon would vanifh, if the world were blefs'd
With facred love, by which they are reprefs'd.   20
  Impendent death, and guilt that threatens hell,
Are dreadful guefts, which here with mortals dwell;
And a vex'd confcience, mingling with their joy
Thoughts of defpair does their whole life annoy;
But love appearing, all thofe terrors fly;   25
We live contented, and contented die.
They in whofe breaft this facred love has place,
Death as a paffage to their joy embrace.
Clouds and thick vapours, which obfcure the day,
The fun's victorious beams may chafe away: 30
Thofe which our life corrupt and darken, love
(The nobler ftar!) muft from the foul remove.
Spots are obferv'd in that which bounds the year;
This brighter fun moves in a boundlefs fphere,
Of heav'n the joy, the glory, and the light;
Shines among angels, and admits no night.   36

CANTO V.

Tʜɪs Iron Age (fo fraudulent and bold!)
Touch'd with this love, would be an Age of Gold :
Not, as they feign'd, that oaks fhould honey drop,
Or land neglected bear an unfown crop ;
Love would make all things eafy, fafe, and cheap ;   5
None for himfelf would either fow or reap:
Our ready help and mutual love would yield
A nobler harvefl than the richefl field.
Famine and death, confin'd to certain parts,
Extended are by barrennefs of hearts.   10
Some pine for want where others furfeit now;
But then we fhould the ufe of plenty know.
Love would betwixt the rich and needy ftand,
And fpread Heav'n's bounty with an equal hand :
At once the givers and receivers blefs,   15
Increafe their joy, and make their fuff'ring lefs.
Who for himfelf no miracle would make,
Difpens'd with fev'ral for the people's fake :
He that, long fafting, would no wonder fhow,
Made loaves and fifhes, as they ate them, grow.   20
Of all his pow'r, which boundlefs was above,
Here he us'd none but to exprefs his love;
And fuch a love would make our joy exceed,
Not when our own, but other mouths we feed.

   Laws would be ufelefs which rude nature awe;   25
Love, changing nature, would prevent the law :

Tigers and lions into dens we thruſt,
But milder creatures with their freedom truſt.
Devils are chain'd, and tremble; but the Spouſe
No force but love, nor bond but bounty, knows. 30
Men (whom we now ſo fierce and dang'rous ſee)
Would guardian angels to each other be:
Such wonders can this mighty love perform,
Vultures to doves, wolves into lambs transform!
Love what Iſaiah prophefy'd can do,   35
Exalt the vallies, lay the mountains low,
Humble the lofty, the dejeĉted raiſe,
Smooth and make ſtraight our rough and crooked ways.
Love, ſtrong as death, and like it, levels all;
With that poſſeſt, the great in title fall: 40
Themſelves eſteem but equal to the leaſt,
Whom Heav'n with that high charaĉter has bleſt.
This love, the centre of our union, can
Alone beſtow complete repoſe on man;
Tame his wild appetite, make inward peace,   45
And foreign ſtrife among the nations ceaſe.
No martial trumpet ſhould diſturb our reſt,
Nor princes arm, tho' to ſubdue the Eaſt,
Where for the tomb ſo many heroes (taught
By thoſe that guided their devotion) fought.   50
Thrice-happy we, could we like ardour have
To gain his love, as they to win his grave!
Love as he lov'd! A love ſo unconfin'd,
With arms extended, would embrace mankind.

Self-love would ceafe, or be dilated, when 　　55
We fhould behold as many felfs as men;
All of one family, in blood ally'd,
His precious blood, that for our ranfom dy'd! 　　58

CANTO VI.

Tho' the creation (fo divinely taught!)
Prints fuch a lively image on our thought,
That the firft fpark of new-created light,
From Chaos ftrook, affects our prefent fight,
Yet the firft Chriftians did efteem more bleft 　　5
The day of rifing than the day of reft,
That ev'ry week might new occafion give
To make his triumph in their mem'ry live.
Then let our Mufe compofe a facred charm
To keep his blood among us ever warm, 　　10
And finging as the bleffed do above,
With our laft breath dilate this flame of love.
But on fo vaft a fubject who can find
Words that may reach th' ideas of his mind?
Our language fails; or, if it could fupply, 　　15
What mortal thought can raife itfelf fo high?
Defpairing here, we might abandon art,
And only hope to have it in our heart.
But tho' we find this facred tafk too hard,
Yet the defign, th' endeavour, brings reward. 　　20
The contemplation does fufpend our woe,
And makes a truce with all the ills we know.

As Saul's afflicted spirit from the found
Of David's harp a prefent folace found;
So on this theme while we our Mufe engage,   25
No wounds are felt of Fortune or of Age.
On Divine Love to meditate is peace,
And makes all care of meaner things to ceafe.
    Amaz'd at once, and comforted, to find
A boundlefs Pow'r fo infinitely kind, .   30
The foul contending to that light to flee
From her dark cell, we practife how to die;
Employing thus the poet's winged art,
To reach this love, and grave it in our heart.
Joy fo complete, fo folid, and fevere,   35
Would leave no place for meaner pleafures there;
Pale they would look, as ftars that muft be gone,
When from the Eaft the rifing fun comes on.   38

OF THE FEAR OF GOD.

CANTO I.

The fear of God is freedom, joy, and peace,
And makes all ills that vex us here to ceafe.
Tho' the word Fear, fome men may ill endure,
'Tis fuch a fear as only makes fecure.
Afk of no angel to reveal thy fate;   5
Look in thy heart, the mirror of thy ftate.
He that invites will not th' invited mock,
Op'ning to all that do in earneft knock.
Our hopes are all well-grounded on this fear;
All our affurance rolls upon that fphere.   10
This fear, that drives all other fears away,
Shall be my fong the morning of our day!
Where that fear is there's nothing to be fear'd:
It brings from heav'n an angel for a guard.
Tranquillity and peace this fear does give;   15
Hell gapes for thofe that do without it live.
It is a beam which he on man lets fall
Of light, by which he made and governs all.
'Tis God alone fhould not offended be;
But we pleafe others, as more great than he.   20
For a good caufe the fufferings of man
May well be borne: 'tis more than angels can.
Man, fince his fall, in no mean ftation refts,
Above the angels, or below the beafts

He with true joy their hearts does only fill,   25
That thirst and hunger to perform his will.
Others, tho' rich, shall in this world be vext,
And sadly live, in terror of the next.
The world's great conqu'ror * would his point pursue,
And wept becaufe he could not find a new;   30
Which had he done, yet still he would have cry'd,
To make him work until a third he fpy'd.
Ambition, avarice, will nothing owe
To Heav'n itfelf, unlefs it make them grow.
Tho' richly fed, man's care does still exceed;   35
Has but one mouth, yet would a thoufand feed.
In wealth and honour, by fuch men poffeft,
If it increafe not, there is found no reft.
All their delight is while their wifh comes in;
Sad when it ftops, as there had nothing been.   40
'Tis ftrange men fhould neglect their prefent ftore,
And take no joy but in purfuing more;
No! tho' arriv'd at all the world can aim;
This is the mark and glory of our frame.
A foul capacious of the Deity,   45
Nothing but he that made can fatisfy.
A thoufand worlds, if we with him compare,
Lefs than fo many drops of water are.
Men take no pleafure but in new defigns;
And what they hope for what they have outfhines.   50
Our fheep and oxen feem no more to crave,
With full content feeding on what they have;

         * Alexander.

Vex not themfelves for an increafe of ftóre,
But think to-morrow we fhall give them more.
What we from day to day receive from Heav'n,   55
They do from us expect it fhould be giv'n.
We made them not, yet they on us rely,
More than vain men upon the Deity;
More beafts than they! that will not underftand
That we are fed from his immediate hand.   60
Man, that in him has being, moves, and lives,
What can he have or ufe but what he gives?
So that no bread can nourifhment afford,
Or ufeful be, without his Sacred Word.   64

CANTO II.

EARTH praifes conquerors for fhedding blood,
Heav'n thofe that love their foes, and do them good.
It is terreftrial honour to be crown'd
For ftrowing men, like rufhes, on the ground.
True glory 'tis to rife above them all,   5
Without the advantage taken by their fall.
He that in fight diminifhes mankind,   !
Does no addition to his ftature find;
But he that does a noble nature fhow,
Obliging others, ftill does higher grow: 10
For virtue practis'd fuch an habit gives,
That among men he like an angel lives:
Humbly he doth, and without envy, dwell,
Lov'd and admir'd by thofe he does excel.

Fools anger fhew, which politicians hide;   15
Bleft with this fear, men let it not abide.
The humble man, when he receives a wrong,
Refers revenge to whom it doth belong:
Nor fees he reafon why he fhould engage,
Or vex his fpirit, for another's rage.   20
Plac'd on a rock, vain men he pities, toft
On raging waves, and in the tempeft loft.
The rolling planets, and the glorious fun,
Still keep that order which they firft begun:
They their firft leffon conftantly repeat,   25
Which their Creator as a law did fet.
Above, below, exactly all obey;
But wretched men have found another way:
Knowledge of good and evil, as at firft,
(That vain perfuafion!) keeps them ftill accurft! 30
The Sacred Word refufing as a guide,
Slaves they become to luxury and pride.
As clocks, remaining in the fkilful hand
Of fome great mafter, at the figure ftand,
But when abroad, neglected they do go,   35
At random ftrike, and the falfe hour do fhow;
So from our Maker wandering, we ftray,
Like birds that know not to their nefts the way.
In him we dwelt before our exile here,
And may, returning, find contentment there: 40
True joy may find, perfection of delight;
Behold his face, and fhun eternal night.

Silence, my Muse! make not thefe jewels cheap,
Expofing to the world too large an heap.
Of all we read the Sacred Writ is beft,   45
Where great truths are in feweft words expreft.
    Wreftling with death, thefe lines I did indite;
No other theme could give my foul delight.
O that my youth had thus employ'd my pen!
Or that I now could write as well as then!   50
But 'tis of grace if ficknefs, age, and pain,
Are felt as throes, when we are born again :
Timely they come to wean us from this earth,
As pangs that wait upon a fecond birth.   54

OF DIVINE POESY.

TWO CANTOS.

Occasioned upon sight of the fifty-third chapter of Isaiah turned into verse by Mrs. Wharton.

CANTO I.

Poets we prize, when in their verse we find
Some great employment of a worthy mind.
Angles have been inquisitive to know
The secret which this oracle does show.
What was to come Isaiah did declare,   5
Which she describes as if she had been there;
Had seen the wounds, which to the reader's view
She draws so lively, that they bleed a-new.
As ivy thrives which on the oak takes hold,
So with the Prophet's may her lines grow old!   10
If they should die, who can the world forgive,
(Such pious lines!) when wanton Sappho's live?
Who with his breath his image did inspire,
Expects it should foment a nobler fire:
Not love which brutes as well as men may know; 15
But love like his to whom that breath we owe.
Verse so design'd, on that high subject wrote,
Is the perfection of an ardent thought;
The smoke which we from burning incense raise,
When we complete the sacrifice of praise.   20

4

In boundlefs verfe the fancy foars too high
For any object but the Deity.
What mortal can with Heav'n pretend to fhare
In the fuperlatives of wife and fair?
A meaner fubject when with thefe we grace,   25
A giant's habit on a dwarf we place.
Sacred fhould be the product of our Mufe,
Like that fweet oil, above all private ufe,
On pain of death forbidden to be made,
But when it fhould be on the altar laid.   30
Verfe fhews a rich ineftimable vein,
When dropp'd from heav'n 'tis thither fent again.
    Of bounty 'tis that he admits onr praife,
Which does not him, but us that yield it, raife:
For as that angel up to heav'n did rife,   35
Borne on the flame of Manoah's facrifice;
So, wing'd with praife, we penetrate the fky,
Teach clouds and ftars to praife him as we fly;
The whole creation, (by our fall made groan!)
His praife to echo, and fufpend their moan.   · 40
For that he reigns all creatures fhould rejoice,
And we with fongs fupply their want of voice.
The church triumphant, and the church below,
In fongs of praife their prefent union fhow:
Their joys are full; our expectation long;   45
In life we differ, but we join in fong.
Angels and we, affifted by this art,
May fing together, tho' we dwell a-part.
    Volume II.   K

Thus we reach heav'n, while vainer poems muft
No higher rife than winds may lift the duft.   50
From that they fpring; this from his breath that gave,
To the firft duft, th' immortal foul we have.
His praife well fung, (our great endeavour here)
Shakes off the duft, and makes that breath appear. 54

CANTO II,

He that did firft this way of writing grace *,
Convers'd with the Almighty face to face:
Wonders he did in facred verfe unfold,
When he had more than eighty winters told.
The writer feels no dire effect of age,   5
Nor verfe, that flows from fo divine a rage.
Eldeft of poets, he beheld the light,
When firft it triumph'd o'er eternal night ;
Chaos he faw, and could diftinctly tell
How that confufion into order fell.   10
As if confulted with, he has expreft
The work of the Creator, and his reft;
How the flood drown'd the firft offending race,
Which might the figure of our globe deface.
For new-made earth, fo even and fo fair,   15
Lefs equal now, uncertain makes the air;
Surpris'd with heat and unexpected cold,
Early diftempers make our youth look old:
Our days fo evil, and fo few, may tell
That on the ruins of that world we dwell.   20

* Mofes,

Strong as the oaks that nourifh'd them, and high,
That long-liv'd race did on their force rely,
Neglecting Heav'n ; but we of fhorter date !
Should be more mindful of impendent fate.
To worms that crawl upon this rubbifh here,   25
This fpan of life may yet too long appear :
Enough to humble, and to make us great,
If it prepare us for a nobler feat.
Which well obferving, he, in numerous lines,
Taught wretched man how faft his life declines : 30
In whom he dwelt before the world was made,
And may again retire when that fhall fade.
The lafting Iliads have not liv'd fo long
As his and Deborah's triumphant fong.
Delphos unknown, no Mufe could them infpire   35
But that which governs the celeftial choir.
Heav'n to the pious did this art reveal,
And from their ftore fuccceding poets fteal.
Homer's Scamander for the Trojans fought,
And fwell'd fo high, by her old Kifhon taught, 40
His river fcarce could fierce Achilles ftay ;
Her's, more fuccefsful, fwept her foes away.
The hoft of heaven, his Phœbus and his Mars,
He arms, inftructed by her fighting ftars.
She led them all againft the common foe ;   45
But he (mifled by what he faw below !)
The pow'rs above, like wretched men, divides,
And breaks their union into diff'rent fides.

The noblest parts which in his heroes shine,
May be but copies of that heroine.·   ,   50
Homer himself, and Agamemnon, she
The writer could, and the commander, be.
Truth she relates in a sublimer strain,
Than all the tales the boldest Greeks could feign;
For what she sung that spirit did indite,   55
Which gave her courage and success in fight.
A double garland crowns the matchless dame;
From Heav'n her poem and her conquest came.

   Tho' of the Jews she merit most esteem,
Yet here the Christian has the greater theme: 60
Her martial song describes how Sis'ra fell;
This sings our triumph over death and hell.
The rising light employ'd the sacred breath ·
Of the blest Virgin and Elisabeth.
In songs of joy the angels' sung his birth :   65
Here how he treated was upon the earth
Trembling we read! th' affliction and the scorn,
Which for our guilt so patiently was borne !
Conception, birth, and suff'ring, all belong,
(Tho' various parts) to one celestial song;   70
And she, well using so divine an art,
Has in this consort sung the tragic part.

   As Hannah's seed was vow'd to sacred use,
So here this lady consecrates her Muse.
With like reward may Heav'n her bed adorn,
With fruit as fair as by her Muse is born!   76

PARAPHRASE ON THE LORD'S PRAYER

Silence, you Winds! liften, ethereal Lights!
While our Urania fings what Heav'n indites:
The numbers are the nymph's; but from above
Defcends the pledge of that eternal love.
Here wretched mortals have not leave alone,   5
But are inftructed to approach his throne;
And how can he to miferable men
Deny requefts which his own hand did pen?
   In the Evangelifts we find the profe
Which, paraphras'd by her, a poem grows;   10
A devout rapture! fo divine a hymn,
It may become the higheft feraphim!
For they, like her, in that celeftial choir,
Sing only what the fpirit does infpire.
Taught by our Lord and theirs, with us they may
For all but pardon for offences pray.   16

F. iij

I. His facred name with reverence profound
Should mention'd be, and trembling at the found!
It was Jehovah; 'tis Our Father now;
So low to us does Heav'n vouchfafe to bow *!
He brought it down that taught us how to pray,   5
And did fo dearly for our ranfom pay.

II. *His kingdom come.* For this we pray in vain,
Unlefs he does in our affections reign.
Abfurd it were to wifh for fuch a King,
And not obedience to his fceptre bring,   10
Whofe yoke is eafy, and his burthen light, ·
His fervice freedom, and his judgments right.

III. *His will be done.* In fact 'tis always done;
But, as in heav'n, it muft be made our own.
His will fhould all our inclinations fway,   15
Whom Nature and the univerfe obey.
Happy the man! whofe wifhes are confin'd
To what has been eternally defign'd;
Referring all to his paternal care,
To whom more dear than to ourfelves we are.   20

IV. It is not what our avarice hoards up;
'Tis he that feeds us, and that fills our cup:

* Pfalm xviii. 9.

Like new-born babes depending on the breaft,
From day to day we on his bounty feaft:
Nor fhould the foul expect above a day   25
To dwell in her frail tenement of clay:
The fetting fun fhould feem to bound our race,
And the new day a gift of fpecial grace.

 V. *That he fhould all our trefpaffes forgive,*
While we in hatred with our neighbours live :   30
Tho' fo to pray may feem an eafy tafk,
We curfe ourfelves when thus inclin'd we afk.
This pray'r to ufe, we ought with equal care
Our fouls, as to the facrament, prepare.
The nobleft worfhip of the Pow'r above,   35
Is to extol and imitate his love;
Not to forgive our enemies alone,
But ufe our bounty that they may be won.

 VI. *Guard us from all temptations of the foe ;*
And thofe we may in feveral ftations know :   40
The rich and poor in flipp'ry places ftand.
Give us enough! but with a fparing hand !
Not ill-perfuading want, nor wanton wealth,
But what proportion'd is to life and health :
For not the dead but living fing thy praife,
Exalt thy kingdom, and thy glory raife.   46

  Favete linguis! • • • •
  Virginibus puerifque canto.   Hor.

WHEN we for age could neither read nor write,
The subject made us able to indite :
The soul, with nobler resolutions deckt,
The body stooping, does herself erect.
No mortal parts are requisite to raise   5
Her that, unbody'd, can her Maker praise.

   The seas are quiet when the winds give o'er :
So, calm are we when passions are no more!
For then we know how vain it was to boast
Of fleeting things, so certain to be lost.   10
Clouds of affection from our younger eyes
Conceal that emptiness which age descries.

   The soul's dark cottage, batter'd and decay'd,
Lets in new light thro' chinks that time has made :
Stronger by weakness, wiser men become,   15
As they draw near to their eternal home.
Leaving the old, both worlds at once they view,
That stand upon the threshold of the new.   18.

        * * * * Miratur limen Olympi.   Virg.

OBSERVATIONS[*].

ONE of our moſt celebrated writers, both for learning and language, has defined ſatire and invective to
be the eaſieſt kind of wit, becauſe almoſt any degree
of it will ſerve to abuſe and find fault: " for wit,
" (ſays he) is a keen inſtrument, and every one can
" cut and gaſh with it; but to carve a beautiful image,
" and poliſh it, requires great art and dexterity. To
" praiſe any thing well is an argument of much more
" wit than to abuſe. A little wit, and a great deal of
" ill-nature, will furniſh a man for ſatire; but the
" greateſt inſtance of wit is to commend well. And,
" perhaps, the beſt things are the hardeſt to be duly
" commended; for though there be a great deal of
" matter to work upon, yet there is great judgment
" required to make choice; and where the ſubject is
" great and excellent, it is hard not to ſink below
" the dignity of it." Whether or not Dr. Tillotſon
had Mr. Waller in his thoughts when he was giving
this deſcription of wit, it is evident that he has, in
the livelieſt colours, delineated the character of his
genius and writings. And ſince it was his principal
intention to recommend, with all the ornaments of
poetry, the brighteſt examples of his own age to the
imitation of all that ſhould ſucceed and even deſired
that every verſe might be expunged which did not

* Excerpted from Mr. Fenton's Quarto edition of 1729.

imply fome motive to virtue, I believe it will be fer-
viceable to many of his admirers, in a few curfory Remarks, to give an account of the occafions on which
fome of his poems were written, and the characters
of the perfons to whom others were addreffed: many
of which, at the diftance of an hundred years, muft
be grown obfcure to moft of his readers. Nor fhall I
be much concerned at the cenfure of thofe who may
think I have beftowed too much pains on a modern
poet of our own nation, before I am convinced that
we owe lefs to the memory of Mr. Waller, than Italy
and France have long fince paid to their Petrarch
and Malherbe; the former of whom is faid to have
employed as many commentators as even Virgil himfelf: and not only the learned Menage, but all the
French Academy, thought the latter highly deferved
their confideration.

VOL. I.

MISCELLANIES.

*Of the danger his Majefty (being Prince) efcaped in the
road at St. Andero, p. 57.*

This poem may ferve as a model for thofe who intend to fucceed in panegyric, in which our Author
illuftrates a plain hiftorical fact with all the graces of
poetical fiction; as will appear by comparing it with

the fubject, as the writers of that age have left it recorded. Prince Charles having fpent about fix months
at Madrid in foliciting a marriage with the Infanta
of Spain, was at length difgufted with the affected
delays which he met with in that court, and refolved
on returning to England. The royal navy, under the
command of the Earl of Rutland, being arrived in the
Bay of Bifcay, at the port of St. Andero, he was attended from Madrid by the Cardinal Zapata, the
Marquis Aytone, the Earls of Gondemar, Monterie,
Baraias, and other grandees, whom the Prince entertained magnificently on fhipboard; but in carrying
them back to fhore, a tempeft overtook them with fo
much fury, that they could neither reach land nor regain the fleet; and night coming on when the rowers
were fainting with toil, their horror was almoft in-
creafed to defpair. In this calamity they yielded themfelves to the mercy of the feas, till, at laft, they fpied
a light in a fhip, near to which the ftorm had driven
them, on which, not without much danger of being
dafhed to pieces, they were fafely received; and when
the tempeft abated, his Highnefs returned to the Admiral, and arrived at Portfmouth on the 5th of Oc-
tober 1623, when (as our Englifh Cicero expreffeth
it) the whole nation feemed for joy to go out beyond
its own fhores to meet him. This adventure happen-
ed in the eighteenth year of Mr. Waller's age; by
which it appears that he began to write only twenty-

five years after the death of Spenfer, of whom I fhall fay fomething more in the courfe of thefe Obfervations.

*Of his Majefty's receiving the news of the Duke of Buck-
    ingham's death, p. 63.*

GEORGE VILLIERS, Duke of Buckingham, was a perfon whom Nature feemed to have folicitoufly intended for a court, and Fortune was equally induftrious
to accomplifh her intentions. At his firft appearance
there he was received with the fmile of K. James I.
who, from the ftation of a private gentleman, in a
few years advanced him to all the dignities that even
himfelf could defire; and no other perfon was employed in any eminent poft, who did not owe their rife
to, or their dependence entirely upon, him. By a fingular felicity he preferved and improved the fame intereft with K. Charles I.; fo that the crown of England, upon whatever head it fhone, feemed to have
been deftined to reflect a luftre on his fortune. In this
career of profperity he gave the rein to many crimi-
nal paffions, and thought nothing unlawful that could
gratify his luft, his ambition, or his revenge, which
precipitated him into many unpopular and unjuftifi-
able actions, by which, at length, he became odious to
the nation; till Providence fuffered him to be cut off
in the full ftrength and verdure of his age (for he had
not exceeded the thirty-fixth year) by the vulgar

hand of a melancholic aſſaſſin. The perſon was one Lieut. Felton, who apprehended himſelf injured by the Duke, who, upon the vacancy of a captain's com- miſſion, had placed another in that poſt, to which Felton thought that his ſervices entitled him. Ac- cordingly, to accompliſh his revenge, when the Duke was at Portſmouth, ready to embark on board the fleet that was to relieve Rochelle, the Lieutenant pur- ſued him thither, where waiting an opportunity to perpetrate his horrid deſign, at the firſt that offered it- ſelf he ſtabbed him to the heart; the court being then at Southwick, the ſeat of Sir Daniel Norton, about five miles diſtant from the ſcene where this tragedy was acted. The King's behaviour on this occaſion is the ſubject of Mr. Waller's poem. The Duke having been murdered on the 23d of Auguſt 1628, it is evident that Mr. Waller wrote this poem *anno ætat.* 23.

On the taking of Salle, *p. 65.*

SALLE is a city in the province of Fez, and derives its name from the river Sala, on which it is ſituated, near its influx into the Atlantic ocean. It was a place of good commerce, till addicting itſelf entirely to pi- racy, and revolting from its allegiance to the Empe- ror of Morocco, in the year 1632 he ſent an embaſſy to King Charles, deſiring him to ſend a ſquadron of men of war to lie before the town whilſt he attacked

It by land; which the King confenting to, the city
was foon reduced. the fortifications demolifhed, and
the leaders of the rebellion put to death. The year
following the Emperor fent another ambaffador with
a prefent of fine Barbary horfes, and three hundred
Chriftian flaves; at the fame time defiring his Majefty, that " fince it had pleafed God to be fo aufpi-
" cious to their beginning, in the conqueft of Salle,
" they might join and fucceed, with hope of like fuc-
" cefs, in war againft Tunis, Algier, and other pla-
" ces, dens and receptacles for the inhuman villanies
" of thofe that abhor rule and government." From
" whence it appears that Mr. Waller wrote this poem
anno ætat. 28.

Puerperium, p. 73.

As far as we are able to guefs, at this diftance, Mr.
Waller feems to have written this poem in the year
1640, *anno ætat.* 35, before the Queen was delivered,
at Oatlands, of her fourth fon, Henry Duke of Gloucefter, while the Scots were marching into England.

The Countefs of Carlifle in mourning, p. 74.

To form a juft idea of the perfon whofe death occafioned the writing of thefe verfes, it will be neceffary
to perufe his character, as it is drawn by the Earl of

Clarendon, whom on all occasions I shall employ to
set Mr. Waller's Poems in a clearer light; and I pre-
sume, if Thucydides and Livy could have been made
as serviceable in illustrating the Greek and Roman
Classics, the world would never have accused their edi-
tors of being too sparing of their own speculations.

    " He was a younger brother of a noble family in
" Scotland, and came into the kingdom with King
" James, as a gentleman, under no other character than
" a person well qualified by his breeding in France,
" and by study in human learning, in which he bore
" a good part in the entertainment of the King, who
" much delighted in that exercise; and by these means,
" and notable gracefulness in his behaviour, and affa-
" bility, in which he excelled, he had wrought him-
" self into a particular interest with his master, and
" into greater affection and esteem with the whole
" English nation, than any other of that country,
" by chusing their friendships and conversation, and
" really preferring it to any of his own; insomuch
" as, upon the King's making him Gentleman of his
" Bedchamber, and Viscount Doncaster, by his royal
" mediation (in which office he was a most prevalent
" prince) he obtained the sole daughter and heir of
" the Lord Denny to be given him in marriage; by
" which he had a fair fortune in land provided for
" any issue he should raise, and which his son, by this
" lady, lived long to enjoy. He ascended, afterwards,

" and with the expedition he defired, to the other
" conveniencies of the court. He was Groom of the
" Stole, and an Earl, and Knight of the Garter; and
" married a beautiful young lady, daughter to the
" Earl of Northumberland, without any other appro-
" bation of her father, or concernment in it, than
" suffering him and her to come into his presence af-
" ter they were married. He lived rather in a fair in-
" telligence than any friendship with the favourites,
" having credit enough with his mafter to provide for
" his own intereft, and he troubled not himself for
" that of other men; and had no other confideration
" of money than for the fupport of his luftre; and
" whilft he could do that he cared not for money,
" having no bowels in the point of running in debt,
" or borrowing all he could. He was furely a man of
" the greateft expenfe, in his own perfon, of any in the
" age he lived, and introduced more of that expenfe,
" in the excefs of clothes and diet, than any other
" man; and was indeed the original of all thofe in-
" ventions from which others did but tranfcribe co-
" pies. He had a great univerfal underftanding, and
" could have taken as much delight in any other way,
" if he had thought any other as pleafant, and worth
" his care; but he found bufinefs was attended with
" more rivals and vexations, and, he thought, with
" much lefs pleafure, and not more innocence. He
" left behind him the reputation of a very fine gen-

" then   ; and a moſt accompliſhed courtier ; and after
" having ſpent, in a very jovial life, above 400,000 *l.*
" which, upon a ſtrict computation, he received from
" the crown, he left not a houſe nor acre of land to be,
" remembered by. And when he had in his proſpect
" (for he was very ſharp-ſighted, and ſaw as far be-
" fore him as moſt men) the gathering together of
" that cloud in Scotland, which ſhortly after cover-
" ed both kingdoms, he died with as much tranquil-
" lity of mind, to all appearance, as uſed to attend a
" man of more ſevere exerciſe of virtue, and with as
" little apprehenſion of death, which he expected
" many days."

His expenſive luxury has been juſt now mentioned in the Earl of Clarendon's character, to which I
will add what is recorded by Oſborn, who was like-
wiſe his contemporary. " The Earl of Carliſle," ſays
he, " was one of the quorum that brought in the va-
" nity of ante-ſuppers, not heard of in our forefa-
" thers' time, and, for ought I have read, or at leaſt
" remember, unpractiſed by the moſt luxurious ty-
" rants; the manner of which was, to have the board
" covered at the firſt entrance of the gueſts with diſhes
" as high as a tall man could well reach, filled with
" the choiceſt and deareſt viands ſea or land could
" afford ; and all this once ſeen, and having feaſted
" the eyes of the invited, was in a manner thrown
" away, and freſh ſet on to the ſame height, having

" only this advantage of the other, that it was hot.
" I cannot forget one of the attendants of the King
" that, at a feaſt made by this monſter in exceſs, ate;
" to his ſingle ſhare, a whole pie, reckoned to my Lord
" at 10 *l.* another writer ſays at 20 *l.*" * *.* What fol-
lows is too coarſe to be tranſcribed, till he comes to
tell us * * * " When the moſt able phyſicians, and the·
" Earl's own weakneſs, had paſſed judgment he could
" not live many days, he did not forbear his entertain-
" ments, but made divers brave clothes (as he ſaid)
" to outface naked and deſpicable Death withal ;
" blaſpheming God ſo far in the perſon of his hand-
" maid Nature, as to ſay ſhe wanted wiſdom, love,
" or power, in making man mortal, and ſubject to
" diſeaſes; forgetting that if every individual his
" own luſt had been able to have produced ſhould
" have proſecuted an equal exceſs with his, they
" would, in a far leſs time than an age, have brought
" themſelves or the world into the ſame diſeaſe he
" died of, which was a conſumption."

In anſwer to one who writ a libel againſt the Counteſs of
Carliſle, p. 76.

THE title of this poem is ſupplied from the table to
the firſt edition : the beginning of it refers to a paſ-
ſage in the fifth Iliad, where Homer introduceth Pallas inſpiriting Diomede to wound Venus, when ſhe
was reſcuing her ſon Æneas from imminent danger
in a combat. . ·

On my Lady Dorothy Sidney's picture, p. 78.

ROBERT SIDNEY, the second of that name who suc-
ceeded to the Earldom of Leicester, married the Lady Dorothy Percy, sister to the celebrated Countess
of Carlisle, by whom he had a numerous issue. Of
eight daughters, the Lady Dorothy, whom Mr. Waller has made immortal in his Poems, was the first-
born; but when or where she was born I have not
been able to discover, no mention being made of her
name in the register at Penshurst : so that, like the
Grecian Venus, (whom the Muses, I think, never pretended to have seen in her cradle) she appears at
once in the full bloom and lustre of beauty, to receive
the hymns of her adorers.

Non licuit populis parvam te, Diva, videre.

In the year 1639 she was married to Henry Lord
Spenser, created Earl of Sunderland by K. Charles I.
in whose cause, a little more than four years after his
marriage, he was slain at the battle of Newbury, before he had completed the twenty-third year of his
age. "A lord of great fortune, and early judgment !
" who having no command in the army, attended
" upon the King's person under the obligation of
" honour; and putting himself, that day, (Sept, 20.
" 1643) in the King's troop a volunteer, before they
" came to charge was taken away by a cannon bullet."

By this lady he left three children, only one of which was a fon, from whom the prefent Earl of Sunderland is lineally defcended; and having furvived her lord about forty years, fhe was buried in the fame vault with him, at Brinton in Northamptonfhire, on the 25th of February 1683.

Such was Philoclea, and fuch Dorus' flame !] This verfe is reftored to its native purity from the edition that was printed in the year 1645.

At Penfhurft, p. 79.

The name of this feat denotes its fituation to be in a woody country, which is the extremity of the Wealde of Kent, to which Mr. Waller has alluded:

Embroider'd fo with flowers where fhe ftood,
That it became a garden of a wood.

In the reign of K. Edward VI. it was forfeited to the crown by its former proprietor, and granted by that Prince to Sir William Sidney, Lord Chamberlain of his Houfehold.

Had Dorethea liv'd, &c.] This verfe is printed as it ftands in the old edition; by which the poem appears to have been written before Mr. Waller had determined to celebrate this lady under the name of Sacharifla, a name which recalls to mind what is related of the Turks, who, in their gallantries, think *fucar birpara, i. e.* bit of fugar, to be the moft polite and endearing compliment they can ufe to the ladies.

The story of Phœbus and Daphne applied, p. 84.

THE paffion of Apollo for Daphne is related by Ovid, in the firft book of his Metamorphofes, the application of which has produced one of the moft beautiful poems in our own or any other modern language. Yet I cannot think Mr. Waller was fo peculiarly fond of it as likewife to be author of the following verfion, but rather give credit to a memorandum which I once found in the margin of an old edition, which affirmed that Sir John Suckling tranflated it into Latin.

So in thofe nations which the fun adore, &c.] This fimile is reftored from the edition that was printed in the year 1645; in all others it is omitted.

Upon the death of my Lady Rich, p. 90.

IN all Mr. Waller's collection of beauties, no one appears more amiable in all lights than fhe whofe untimely death is deplored in this excellent elegy. She was the Lady Anne Cavendifh, fole daughter of William Earl of Devonfhire, and was married to the heir of that Earl of Warwick whofe character will be recited in thofe Obfervations; by whom fhe left only one fon, who, long after her death, married Cromwell's youngeft daughter. An alliance which, had fhe lived, fhe would no doubt have endeavoured to prevent, as it was moft cordially detefted by all her own loyal relations. Before she had completed the twenty-seventh year of her age, she died at Lees, and was buried at Felsted in Essex, in the year 1638; so that we may conclude Mr. Waller wrote this poem *anno ætat.* 33. A lady! whose accomplishments were in every kind so extraordinary, that they seem to have transcended even his genius to delineate them as they deserved: and therefore I will add another description of her person, from which, when we have formed an idea of consummate beauty and virtue, and applied it to my Lady Rich, we shall not flatter her memory. The verses were written by Mr. Sidney Godolphin, a young gentleman of extraordinary parts, who, in an engagement with the rebels in the west, was slain at Chagford, a little town in the south of Devon, leaving the misfortune of his death upon a place which could never otherwise have had a mention to the world.

> Possess'd of all that Nature could bestow,
> All we can wish to be, or reach to know;
> Equal to all the patterns which our mind
> Can frame of good beyond the good we find;
> All beauties which have pow'r to bless the sight,
> Mix'd with transparent virtue's greater light;
> At once producing love and reverence,
> The admiration of the soul and sense;
> The most discerning thoughts, the calmest breast,
> Most apt to pardon, needing pardon least;
> The largest mind, and which did most extend
> To all the laws of daughter, wife, and friend;
> The most allow'd example, by what line
> To live, what path to follow, what decline;

Who beft all diftant virtues reconcil'd,
Strict, cheerful, humble, great, fevere, and mild ;
Conflantly pious to her lateft breath,
Not more a pattern in her life than death ;
The Lady Rich lies here. More frequent tears
Have never honour'd any tomb than her's.

Save that fhe grac'd, &c.] In all the editions it is printed *you grac'd*, as directed to Sachariffa ; but I doubt not of the verfe being originally written as it is here reftored ; for the Lady Dorothy Sidney was not married till about a year after this poem was compofed, and, confequently, a faultlefs wife could be then no part of her character.

Of Mrs. Arden, p. 97.

I suppose fhe was either a Maid of Honour, or a Gentlewoman of the Bedchamber, to K. Charles I.'s Queen, and the fame who is mentioned in the lift of Court ladies who acted Mr. Montague's Shepherd's Paradife, which is defervedly ridiculed by Sir John Suckling in his Seffion of the Poets.

Of the marriage of the Dwarfs, p. 98.

The perfons on whom thefe verfes were written, were Mr. Richard Gibfon, a favourite Page of the Backftairs, and Mrs. Anne Shepherd, whofe marriage King Charles I. honoured with his prefence, and gave the bride. I have feen both of them painted by Sir Peter Lely, and they appeared to have been of an equal ftature, each of them meafuring three feet ten inches. They had nine children, five of which attained to maturity, and were well proportioned to the ufual ftandard of mankind. Mr. Gibfon's genius led him to painting, in the rudiments of which art he was inftructed by De Clein, mafter of the tapeftry works at Mortlack, and famous for the cuts which he defigned for fome of Ogilby's things, and Mr. Sandys's excellent tranflation of Ovid. His paintings in water colours were well efteemed; but the copies which he made of Lely's portraits gained him the greateft reputation. He had the honour to be employed in teaching her late Majefty Queen Anne the art of drawing, and was fent for into Holland to inftruct her fifter the Princefs of Orange. To recompenfe the fhortnefs of their ftature, Nature gave them an equivalent in length of days, for he died in the feventy-fifth year of his age, and his wife, having furvived him almoft twenty years, deceafed *anno Dom.* 1709, *ætat.* 89.

Thyrfis, Galatea, p. 107.

T HE perfon who is the fubject of this poem was the Lady Mary Fielding, daughter to the Earl of Denbeigh, by a fifter of the favourite Duke of Buckingham. She was contracted to the Duke of Hamilton

S

when she was but seven years of age, and in the Memoirs of her lord, written by Burnet, we have her character at large: an author whom I quote the more
willingly on this occasion, presuming his veracity may
pass uncensured, now he happens to speak well of the
dead.

" She was a lady of great and singular worth, and
" her person was noble and graceful, like the hand-
" some race of the Villiers's; but, to such as knew
" her well, the virtues of her mind were far more
" shining. She was educated from a child in the court,
" and esteemed and honoured by all in it, and by
" none more than the late King, (Charles I.) who, as
" he was one of the chastest men, not to say princes,
" so he was a perfect honourer of all virtuous ladies.
" She was lady of the Queen's Bed-chamber, and ad-
" mitted by her Majesty into an intire confidence and
" friendship; and not only was her honour unstained,
" but even her fame continued untouched with ca-
" lumny, she being so strict to the severest rules as
" never to admit of those follies which pass in that
" style for gallantry. She was a most affectionate and
" dutiful wife; and used to say, " she had the greatest
" reason to bless God for having given her such a hus-
" band, whom, as she loved perfectly, so she was not
" ashamed to obey." But that which crowned all her
" other perfections, was the deep sense she had of
" religion. She lived and died in the communion of
Volume II.   M

" the Church of England, and was a very devout per-
" fon. Many years before her death she was so exact
" in obferving her retirements to her clofet, that, not-
" withstanding all her avocations, and the divertife-
" ments of the court, (as the writer was informed by
" one who lived with her) no day paffed over her
" without beftowing large portions of her time on
" them, befides her conftant attendance on the Cha-
" pel. She bore firft three daughters, and then three
" fons. Her daughters were Lady Mary, Lady Anne,
" and Lady Sufanna; her fons were Charles, James,
" and William, but all her fons, and her eldeft daugh-
" ter, died young. A year before fhe died fhe languifh-
" ed, which ended in a confumption, of which, after
" a few months' ficknefs, fhe died; fo that fhe prepa-
" red for death timeoufly. About a month before her
" death fhe called for her children, and gave them
" her laft bleffings and embraces, ordering them to
" be brought no more near her, left the fight of them
" might have kindled too much tendernefs in her
" heart, which fhe was then ftudying to raife above
" all created objects, and fix where fhe was fhortly to
" be admitted. She died the 10th of May 1638, and
" left her lord a moft fad and afflicted perfon; and
" though his fpirit was too great to fink under any
" burthen, yet all his life after he remembered her
" with much tender affection. She died, indeed, in a
" good time for her own repofe, when her lord was

" beginning to engage in the affairs of Scotland,
" which proved fo fatal both to his quiet and life."* * *
From the date of her death, it appears that Mr. Waller wrote this poem *anno ætat.* 33.

Upon Ben. Johnfon, p. 111.

Whatever tradition hath preferved relating to thofe
writers who are celebrated by Mr. Waller, has been
fo often repeated in the Lives of the Englifh Poets, or
mentioned in the *Athenæ Oxonienfes*, that it would be
fuperfluous to tranfcribe what really would yield but
fmall entertainment to the reader; and therefore I
fhall pafs all, or moft of them, over in filence, till I
come to fpeak of my Lord Rofcommon, of whom,
I think, I am enabled to give a fuller account than
has hitherto appeared; and at prefent will only make
this general obfervation on Mr. Waller's commen-
datory verfes, that they are to be efteemed as the
pure effects of candour and friendfhip; in many of
which he feems, like a good-natured magiftrate, to
have been prevailed upon, by the innocent poverty of
the books which he commends, to give them a paff-
port for prefent fubfiftence, in their journey to the
land where all things are forgotten.

Of a war with Spain, and fight at fea, p. 128.

Mr. Waller's principal aim in this poem is to recommend the Protector to the reverence of the nation

under the title of King, which the Ufurper ambiti-
oufly affected : but finding that the fame evil fpirit
which he had artfully conjured up againft his lawful
fovereign ftill poffeffed.the Houfe of Commons to
preplex his own affairs, he projected the fcheme of
engaging in a war with Spain, to be enabled, by foreign
fpoil, to eftablifh his government in what form, and
under what denomination, he pleafed, without depending on parliamentary counfel or fupplies. With
this view he concluded a peace with France againft
Spain, which is cenfured by Ludlow, Wellwood, and
others, for the falfeft ftep he ever made, and the moft
fatal to the tranquillity of Europe. However, his own
hopes were fufficiently anfwered by the fuccefs of that
naval expedition which is the fubject of this poem.

With thefe returns victorious Montagu.] In fome late
editions the title of this poem injurioufly gives the
glory of this action to General Montagu which is
entirely due to Stayner, who, for his bravery on this
occafion, and foon afterwards at Santa Cruz, was
knighted by Cromwell; and had his valour been employed in a better caufe, by a better mafter, he might
have been juftly ranked amongft thofe who have me-
rited moft of the Englifh nation. But when Montagu
came back from the coaft of Portugal, the Marquis's
two fons, and two furviving daughters, with about
ninety other prifoners, and all the bullion, were com-

mitted to his care. With thefe returns he to Portfmouth, where he received the Protector's orders to
bring them by land to London, and his orders were
executed with great oftentation.

Upon the death of the Lord Protector, p. 133.

Mr. Waller wrote this poem *anno ætat.* 53.

Nature herself took notice of his death, &c.] He expired
upon the 3d day of Sept. 1658, a day he thought always very propitious to him, and on which he had
twice triumphed for two of his greateft victories : and
this was now a day very memorable for the greateft
ftorm of wind that had been ever known, for fome
hours before and after his death, which overthrew
trees, houfes, and made great wrecks at fea; and the
tempeft was fo univerfal, that the effects of it were ter-
rible both in France and Flanders, where all people
trembled at it : for befides the wrecks all along the
fea-coaft, many boats were caft away in the very ri-
vers; and within few days after, the circumftance of
his death, that accompanied the ftorm, was univerfally known.

" He was one of thofe men *quos vituperare ne ini-*
" *mici quidem poffunt, nifi ut fimul laudent,* " whom his
" very enemies could not condemn without commend-
" ing him at the fame time :" for he could never
" have done half that mifchief without great courage,

" induſtry, and judgment. He muſt have had a won-
" derful underſtanding in the natures and humours of
" men, and as great a dexterity in applying them,
" who, from a private and obſcure birth, (though of
" a good family) without intereſt or eſtate, alliance
" or friendſhip, could raiſe himſelf to ſuch a height,
" and compound and knead ſuch oppoſite and con-
" tradictory tempers, humours, and intereſts, into a
" conſiſtence that contributed to his own deſigns, and
" to their own deſtruction, whilſt himſelf grew inſen-
" ſibly powerful enough to cut off thoſe by whom he
" had climbed, in the inſtant that they projected to
" demoliſh their own building. What was ſaid of Cin-
" na may, very juſtly be ſaid of him, *Auſum eum, quæ*
" *nemo auderet bonus; perfeciſſe, quæ à nullo niſi fortiſſimo*
" *perfici poſſent:* " he attempted thoſe things which no
" good man durſt have ventured on, and achieved
" thoſe in which none but a valiant and great man
" could have ſucceeded." Without doubt no man
" with more wickedneſs ever attempted any thing,
" or brought to paſs what he deſired more wickedly,
" more in the face and contempt of religion and mo-
" ral honeſty: yet wickedneſs, great as his, could ne-
" ver have accompliſhed thoſe deſigns without the aſ-
" ſiſtance of a great ſpirit, and admirable circumſpec-
" tion and ſagacity, and a moſt magnanimous reſolu-
" tion." *Earl of Clarendon's Hiſtory, Book* xv.

Of the invaſion and defeat of the Turks, p. 139.

THE ſiege of Vienna, which occaſioned the writing
this poem, began about the middle of July 1683, (in
the ſeventy-eighth year of Mr. Waller's age) and was
carried on with great fury by an army of an hundred
thouſand Turks, under the conduct of the Grand Viſier; but he was compelled to raiſe it on the 10th of
the following September, by that heroic prince, John
Sobieſki, king of Poland, at whoſe arrival the Infidels
made ſuch a precipitate flight, that they left behind
them their field-equipage and the ſtandard of the Ot-
toman empire, with an hundred and eighty pieces of
cannon. Upon this defeat the commotions grew ſo
violent among the Janizaries, that the Sultan was obliged to commute for his own ſafety with the death of
his great favourite Cara Muſtapha, the Grand Viſier,
who was ſtrangled at Belgrade on the 25th of December 1683. He had attained to the higheſt dignities
and command that a ſubject is capable of enjoying in
that government, by the intereſt of the Sultaneſs-mo-
ther Valida, to whom, for many years, he had been
a gallant; but not long before this fatal campaign he
had fallen paſſionately in love with Baſch-Lari, the
Sultan's ſiſter, which ſo irritated the forſaken Valida,
that ſhe made uſe of the neceſſities of the ſtate to be
revenged for his inconſtancy, and prevailed with her

fon, the Emperor Mahomet, to fend for his head; to which he is faid to have affented with the greateft reluctance.

Of her Royal Highnefs, mother to the Prince of Orange, &c.
    p. 144.

MARY Princefs of Orange was the eldeft daughter of K. Charles I. born at St James's, *anno Dom.* 1631, and contracted, in the tenth year of her age, to William, only fon of Frederic Henry Prince of Orange. She was a lady whofe piety and incomparable goodnefs of nature were not confined to a fruitlefs compaffion of the calamities of her family, but rendered her active in promoting their interefts, and bountiful to their friends when they wanted her fupport and protection. After nineteen year's abfence fhe returned to her native country, to partake in the general joy at her brother's reftoration. Soon after her arrival the Houfe of Commons prefented her Highnefs with 10,000 *l.* which, though it might in fome meafure evidence their own duty and affection, was but a poor equivalent for only one article of her bounty, fhe having, for many years, appropriated one half of her annual revenue to the fupport of the Duke of Gloucefter, that he might not be influenced to change his religion, by accepting a penfion from the Catholic princes; but her foul was too noble either to balance benéfits herſelf, or to ſuffer others to reduce them to a ſtrict computation. After ſhe had paſſed about three months in England, ſhe died of the ſmall-pox, and was interred in Henry VII.'s chapel, December 31, anno Dom. 1660, ætat ſuæ 29. At the time of his writing this poem Mr. Waller appears to have been in the fifty-fifth year of his age.

Upon her Majeſty's new buildings at Somerſet-houſe, p. 145.

THE queen-mother, Henrietta Maria, returned with a deſign to paſs the remainder of her life in England, anno Dom. 1662, when Mr. Waller was in the fifty-ſeventh year of his age. Upon ſettling at Somerſet-houſe ſhe beautified the old palace, and, I think, added all thoſe buildings that front to the river. Mr. Cowley has an excellent copy of verſes on this occaſion.

Upon the Earl of Roſcommon's tranſlation of Horace, p. 151.

WENTWORTH DILLON, Earl of Roſcommon, was born in Ireland, whilſt the government of that kingdom was committed to the care of the great Earl of Strafford, to whom the Counteſs of Roſcommon (deſcended from the Boyntons of Bramſton, in the county of York) was nearly related; and when he was baptized, the Lord Lieutenant gave him the ſurname of his own family. In that kingdom he paffed the firft years of his infancy; but his father having been converted by Archbifhop Ufher from the communion of the Church of Rome, the Earl of Strafford, apprehending that his family would be expofed to the moft furious effects of religious revenge, at the beginning of the Irifh rebellion, fent for his godfon into England, and placed him at his own feat in Yorkfhire, under the tuition of Dr. Hall, a perfon of eminent learning and piety. By him he was inftructed in Latin; and, without learning the common rules of grammar, which he could never retain in his memory, he attained to write in that language with claffical elegance and propriety, and with fo much eafe, that he chofe it to eqrrefpond with thofe friends who had learning fufficient to fupport the commerce. When the cloud began to gather over England, and the Earl of Strafford was fingled out for a prey to popular fury, by the advice of the Lord Primate Ufher he was fent to complete his education at Caen in Normandy, under the care and direction of the famous Bochartus. After fome years he travelled to Rome, where he grew familiar with the moft valuable remains of Antiquity, applying himfelf particularly to the knowledge of medals, which he gained in perfection, and fpoke Italian with fo much grace and fluency, that he was frequently miftaken there for a native. Soon after the reftoration he returned to England, where he was gracioufly received by K. Charles II. and made Captain of the Band of Penfioners. In the gaieties of that age he was tempted to indulge a violent paffion for gaming, by which he frequently hazarded his life in duels, and exceeded the bounds of a moderate fortune. A difpute with the Lord Privy Seal about part of his eftate obliging him to revifit his native country, he refigned his poft in the Englifh court, and foon after his arrival at Dublin, the Duke of Ormond appointed him to be Captain of the Guards. His beloved Horace obferved, that the difeafes of the mind are feldom cured by change of air, the truth of which was confirmed by his Lordfhip's example; for he was there as much as ever diftempered with the fame fatal affection for play, which engaged him in one adventure that well deferves to be related. As he returned to his lodgings from a gaming-table he was attacked in the dark by three ruffians, who were employed to affaffinate him : the Earl defended himfelf with fo much refolution, that he difpatched one of the aggreffors, whilft a gentleman, accidentally paffing that way, interpofed, and difarmed another; the third fecured himfelf by flight. This generous affiftant was a difbanded officer, of a good family, and fair reputation, who, by what we call the partiality of Fortune, to avoid cenfuring the iniquities of the times, wanted even a plain fuit of clothes to make a decent appearance at the Caftle: but his Lordfhip, on this occafion,

prefenting him to the Duke of Ormond, with great
importunity prevailed with his Grace that he might
refign his poft of Captain of the Guards to his friend;
which for about three years the gentleman enjoyed,
and upon his death the Duke returned the commiffion to his generous benefactor. .

The pleafures of the Englifh court, and the friend-
fhips he had there contracted, were powerful motives
for his return to London. Soon after he came he was
made Mafter of the Horfe to her Royal Highnefs the
Duchefs of York, and married the Lady Frances, eldeft daughter of Richard Earl of Burlington, who before had been the wife of Colonel Courtney. And about
this time, in imitation of thofe learned and polite
affemblies with which he had been acquainted abroad,
particularly one at Caen, (in which his tutor Bochartus died fuddenly whilft he was delivering an oration)
he began to form a fociety for the refining and fix-
ing the ftandard of our language, in which defign his
great friend Mr. Dryden was a principal affiftant: a
defign! of which it is much eafier to conceive an
agreeable idea, than any rational hope ever to fee it
brought to perfection among us. This project, at leaft,
was entirely defeated by the religious commotions
that enfued on King James's acceffion to the throne;
at which time the Earl took a refolution to pafs the
remainder of his life at Rome, telling his friends,
it would be beft to fit next to the chimney when the

2

chamber ſmoked. Amid theſe reflections he was ſeiz-
ed by the gout; and being too impatient of pain, he
permitted a bold French pretender to phyſic to apply
a repelling medicine, in order to give him preſent relief, which drove the diſtemper into his bowels, and
in a ſhort time put a period to his life, in the year
1684. The moment in which he expired he cried out,
with a voice that expreſſed the moſt intenſe fervour of
devotion, .

> My God, my father, and my friend!
> Do not forſake me at my end.

He was buried, with great funeral pomp, in Weſtmin-
ſter Abbey; but his friends ſeem to have thought his
own writings a more durable monument than any they
could erect to his memory. And in them we view the
image of a mind that was naturally ſerious and ſolid,
richly furniſhed and adorned with all the ornaments
of art and ſcience, and thoſe ornaments unaffectedly
diſpoſed in the moſt regular and elegant order. His
imagination might have probably been more fruitful
and ſprightly, if his judgment had been leſs ſevere, but
that ſeverity (delivered in a maſculine, clear, ſuccinct
ſtyle) contributed to make him ſo eminent in the di-
dactical manner, that no man, with juſtice, can affirm
he was ever equalled by any of our own nation, without confeſſing, at the ſame time, that he is inferior to
none. In ſome other kinds of writing his genius ſeems
to have wanted fire to attain the point of perfection:

but who can attain it? Mr. Waller addreſſed this poem to his Lordſhip *anno ætat.* 75.

Ad Comitem Monumetenſem, &c. p. 153.

THIS copy of Latin verſes I found prefixed to the Earl of Monmouth's tranſlation of Cardinal Bentivo- glio's Hiſtory of the Wars of Flanders, which having been publiſhed in the year 1678, we may ſuppoſe that Mr. Waller wrote it *anno ætat.* 73.

On the Duke of Monmouth's expedition into Scotland, &c.
    p. 154.

THE Scots intending to juſtify the barbarous mur- ther of Archbiſhop Sharp by an open rebellion, made their general rendezvous at Bothwell Bridge, where they found their numbers increaſed to about ſeven- teen thouſand men. King Charles having ordered the Duke of Monmouth to ſuppreſs this inſurrection in its infancy, his Grace accordingly repaired to Scotland with almoſt incredible expedition ; and ſoon after his arrival, in one deciſive action, routed and diſperſed the rebels, who left about eight hundred ſlain, and twelve hundred priſoners, behind them. This battle having been fought on the 22d of June 1679, we may conclude that Mr. Waller wrote theſe verſes in the ſeventy-fourth year of his age.

The triple combat, p. 156.

In the year 1675, came over to the English court the famous Duchess of Mazarine, who had formerly the greatest fortune of any lady in Europe, and was judged to have as much merit, at least so far as wit and beauty could extend, the two captivating qualities of her sex. She was once thought a fit match for the King himself, and so designed by the queen-mother, Henrietta Maria, and Cardinal Mazarine; but now, with the loss of her fortune and her reputation, and the final parting from her husband, she was forced to take refuge in the English court, where she was for a while set up as a rival to the Duchess of Portsmouth, and might probably have proved so, had not her amorous inclinations towards another been too soon discovered to the King, who, notwithstanding, allowed her a half pension, 4000 *l.* a-year; and her house, for many years, became the rendezvous of all the men of wit and quality, and the scene of all the news of the Town, of gaming, curious and exquisite entertainments, and all manner of diversions. The reader may find a much fuller character of her in the works of St. Evremond and Abbot St. Real; but this relation from Mr. Echard is sufficient for the present occasion.——I suppose Mr. Waller wrote this poem in the seventieth year of his age.

N ij

Of an elegy made by Mrs. Wharton, &c. p. 157.

SHE was the daughter and co-heiress of Sir Henry Lee of Ditchley, in Oxfordshire, who, having no son, left his estate to be divided between this lady and her sister, the Countess of Abingdon, whose memory Mr Dryden has celebrated in a funeral panegyric. She was the late Marquis of Wharton's first wife, and died without issue. The Earl of Rochester's mother was aunt to her father Sir Henry Lee; for which reason Mr. Waller says, they were allied both in genius and in blood.

Upon our late loss of the Duke of Cambridge, p. 158.

HE was the Duke of York's first son, by his second lady, Mary d'Este, born the 7th of November 1677, and died when he was about a month old.

Instructions to a Painter, &c. p. 159.

I HAVE already observed that Mr. Waller imitated Bufenello's Venetian Triumph in the address of this poem; in which (as, indeed, in most of his panegyrics) he hath so closely confined himself to historical fact, and is so particular and full in describing the whole action, that very few passages will require any explanation. He wrote it *anno ætat.* 60.

The battle of The Summer Iſlands, p. 174.

THE iſlands of Bermuda derived that name from the firſt European diſcoverer, who was a Spaniard; but, about the year 1609, Sir George Summers, being wrecked on that coaſt, ſettled a colony there, which he intended to have planted in Virginia, and called them The Summer Iſlands. They are ſituate in 32 degrees and 30 minutes of northern latitude.

With the ſweet ſound of Sachariſſa's name, &c.] It cannot be ſuppoſed that Mr. Waller would inſinuate any remains of paſſion for the Lady Dorothy after her marriage; the names of Sidney and Sachariſſa were laid down together in 1639; ſo that this poem was certainly written before that year, though there are no hints from which we can diſcover exactly the time of its production. In the concluſion of the laſt poem to that lady he declares his reſolution to make a voyage to divert his deſpair; and if he was a proprietor of The Summer Iſlands, as it is reported he was, he might, perhaps, at that time accompany his friend the Earl of Warwick, who had a large ſhare in that plantation; and that diviſion of Bermuda which was the ſcene of this action which Mr. Waller records, bears the name of that Earl, who, inſtead of loitering away life in court-attendance, employed his younger years in ſettling colonies in the Weſt Indies, an employment more innocent, as well as more honourable,

than what he afterwards engaged in! "He was a man
" of a companionable wit and converfation, of an
" univerfal jollity, and fuch a licenfe in his words and
" in his actions, that a man of lefs virtue could not be
" found out; fo that one might reafonably have be-
" lieved that a man fo qualified would not have been
" able to have contributed much to the overthrow of
" a nation and kingdom : but with all thefe faults he
" had great authority with that people who, in the
" beginning of the troubles, did all the mifchief; and
" by opening his doors, and making his houfe the
" rendezvous of all the filenced minifters, in the time
" when there was authority to filence them; and
" fpending a good part of his eftate (of which he was
" very prodigal) upon them, and by being prefent
" with them at their devotions, and making himfelf
" merry with them, and at them, (which they dif-
" penfed with) he became the head of that party, and
" got the ftyle of *a godly man.* When the King revo-
" ked the Earl of Northumberland's commiffion of
" Admiral, he prefently accepted the office from the
" parliament, and never quitted their ferviee: and
" when Cromwell difbanded that parliament, he be-
" took himfelf to the protection of the Protector,
" married his heir to his daughter, and lived in fo en-
" tire a confidence and friendfhip with him, that
" when he died the Protector exceedingly lamented
" him. He left his eftate (which before was fubject

" to a vaſt debt) more improved and repaired than
" any man who trafficked in that deſperate com-
" modity of Rebellion." *Earl of Clarendon's Hiſtory,*
Book vi.

VOL. II.

EPISTLES.

To the King, on his navy, p. 1.

In all the editions ſince the reſtoration, this poem has
been placed the firſt; which, I ſuppoſe, hath induced
moſt perſons to imagine it to have been written ſeve-
ral years ſooner than it was. In this number I find
the writer of Mr. Waller's life, who believes it was
occaſioned by the fleet that was ſet out under the command of the Lord Viſcount Wimbleton; and ſeems
to have been led into this opinion by that addition to
the title, *in the year* 1626, which has been prefixed in
ſome of the lateſt editions. The gentleman, whoever
he was, that fixed the date of this and ſome other of
the poems, will not appear to have been very compe-
tently qualified for ſuch an undertaking, if we reflect
that he has miſtaken no leſs than two years in his
chronology upon the verſes On the Danger the Prince
eſcaped at St. Andero; and having ſo groſsly erred in
a fact ſo notorious as that, I think we may decently
diſmiſs him from the chair, and hear Mr. Rymer's

opinion, though I believe there is reason not to stand
to his decision in the case depending. "Our language,"
says he, "retained something of the churl; something
" of the stiff and Gothish did stick upon it till long
" after Chaucer. Chaucer threw in Latin, French,
" Provincial, and other languages, like new stum, to
" raise a fermentation. In Queen Elizabeth's time it
" grew fine, but came not to an head and spirit, did
" not shine and sparkle, till Mr. Waller set it a-run-
" ning. And one may observe, by his poem On the
" Navy, *anno* 1632, that not the language only, but
" his poetry, then distinguished him from all his con-
" temporaries, both in England and in other nations,
" and from all before him upwards to Horace and
" Virgil. For there, besides the language, clean and
" majestic; the thoughts new and noble; the verse
" sweet, smooth, full, and strong; the turn of the
" poem is happy to admiration; the first line, with
" all that follow in order, leads to the conclusion;
" all bring to the same point and centre :

> To thee, his chosen, more indulgent, he
> Dares trust such pow'r with so much piety.

" Here is both Homer and Virgil; the *fortis Achilles,*
" and the *pius Æneas,* in the person he compliments,
" and the greatness owing to his virtue. The thought
" and application is most natural, just, and true, in
" poetry, though in fact, and really, he might have no
" more fortitude or piety than another body; for the

" repairing then of Paul's gave a reasonable colour
" for his piety, and that navy-royal might well give
" him the pre-eminence in power above Achilles."

I should willingly have acquiesced in this determination, if there had been any naval armament in the year 1632 confiderable enough for the subject of Mr. Waller's poem; neither did the war betwixt France and Spain, which is referred to in the third verse, break out till, I believe, almost three years after the date that Mr. Rymer hath affigned; and therefore, in a matter that still remains so uncertain, I may venture to interpose my own opinion, which, whether right or no, may be less liable to objections than those that have been already advanced.

In the year 1635 the Hollanders espoused the quarrel of France against Spain, and the terms stipulated in the treaty were, that they should not only divide the provinces of Flanders, but also Dunkirk, Oftend, and the other sea-ports on the coast, equally between them. Upon the concluding this league offensive and defensive, the Dutch forgot their obligations to the crown of England, treated their old benefactors with difrefpect, and were more audacious in their encroachments upon the fishery on our coasts. King Charles thought it was high time to assert his sovereignty over the narrow seas, and immediately fitted out a much greater fleet than had ever been equipped since the reign of Queen Elizabeth, and appointed

the Earl of Lindſey to command it. Sir William Mon-
ſon, who ſerved Vice-admiral under the Earl, informs
us, in his Naval Tracts, that while this fleet was preparing, many idle, factious, and ſcandalous reports
were invented, to perſuade the people that thoſe pre-
parations were only an artifice of ſtate to draw money
from the ſubject. Could Mr. Waller ever have had a
more happy opportunity than this of making his
court to the King, by repreſenting his actions in their
proper light, in proclaiming his navy to be, as in truth
it was, the glory and defence of the nation? And
yet, to deal ingenuouſly, I am of opinion that this
poem was written in the following year, when his
great friend, the Earl of Northumberland, was made
admiral of a fleet not inferior to the former, in the
thirty-firſt year of Mr. Waller's age.

The world's reſtorer once could not endure.] This line
is printed as I find it in the firſt edition; in the others
it is *never cou'd endure.* The building of Babel is related by Moſes in *Geneſis*, chap. xi.

*To the Queen, occaſioned upon ſight of her Majeſty's
    picture, p. 2.*

WHEN all thoughts of a marriage with the Infanta
of Spain were laid aſide, King James conſented that
Prince Charles ſhould make his addreſſes to Henrietta
Maria de Bourbon, youngeſt daughter of Henry IV,

of France, by his queen Mary de Medicis. According-
ingly, in the year 1624, the Lord Kenfington, (afterwards created Earl of Holland) was difpatched to
make propofals to Lewis XIII. by whom they were
embraced, and the nuptial ceremony was performed
in the church of Nôtredame in, Paris, on the 1ft of
May 1625. Mr. Waller feems to have written this
poem foon after her Majefty's arrival in England, *anno
ætat.* 20. Nor fhall we think him too profufe in prai-
fing her beauty, when we read the defcription of her
perfon, which the Lord Kenfington gives, in a letter
to the Prince of Wales, whom he would not dare to
delude with a portrait of his own invention. * * * " Sir,
" if your intentions proceed this way, (as by many
" reafons of ftate and wifdom there is caufe now ra-
" ther to prefs it than flacken it) you will find a lady
" of as much lovelinefs and fweetnefs to deferve your
" affection as any creature under heaven can do. And,
" Sir, by all her fafhions fince my being here, and by
" what I hear from the ladies, it is moft vifible to me
" her infinite value and refpect unto you. Sir, I fay
" not this to betray your belief, but from a true ob-
" fervation and knowledge of this to be fo. I tell you
" this, and muft fomewhat more, in way of admiration
" of the perfon of Madame; for the impreffions I
" had of her were but ordinary, but the amazement
" extraordinary, to find her (as I proteft to God I
" did) the fweeteft creature in France. Her growth

" is very little, fhort of her age, but her wifdom in-
" finitely beyond it. I heard her difcourfe with her
" mother, and the ladies about her, with extraordi-
" nary difcretion and quicknefs. She dances (the
" which I am a witnefs of) as well as ever I faw any
" creature. They fay fhe fings fweetly; I am fure fhe
" looks fo." * * * And in another letter he fays,
" That for beauty and goodnefs fhe was an angel."
This defcription will claim the more regard, when we
reflect on the important occafion on which it was
written, and on the perfon who wrote it, who was
the moft accomplifhed courtier of that age : _elegans
formarum fpectator_, was the Earl of Holland's true character, and it had been happy for himfelf and the nation if he had never afpired to any other.

To the Queen-mother of France, upon her landing, p. 5.

MARY DE MEDICIS, queen-mother of France, is a fad
and very fingular inftance how infecure the moft com-
manding condition may prove againft the viciffitudes
of Fortune. She was daughter to the Great Duke of
Tufcany, wife of Henry IV. of France, mother to
Lewis XIII. his fucceffor, to the Queens of England
and Spain, and to the Duchefs of Savoy, yet was made
a facrifice by her own fon (a timorous and weak prince)
to the ambition of Cardinal Richlieu, to whom fhe
had been a benefactrefs. By him fhe was reprefented

to the King of France as a perfon difaffected to his government, then was perfecuted from the court, and at length confined to Compeigne; from whence fhe made her efcape, the 19th of July 1631, with fo much precipitation, that fhe travelled thirty leagues without taking eafe or refrefhment. In the year 1638, her daughter, the Queen of England, invited her over, to take fanctuary in this nation, whither her evil genius purfued her; for, upon her arrival, the populace raifed a tumult, in which three men were flain; and when the Earl of Holland, who was Lord-lieutenant of Middlefex, gave orders for a guard of a hundred mufqueteers out of the militia to protect her Majefty's perfon, he was anfwered, that they thought it fitter for them to do other things than to guard a foreigner. At length fhe was lodged fafe in St. James's palace, where, for about three years, fhe enjoyed a penfion of 3000 l. a-month. At laft the parliament petitioned for her removal out of the kingdom, which they foftened with a prefent of 10,000 l. to make provifion for her journey. The King's affairs were too much perplexed for him to give protection to others; and therefore, in Auguft 1641, he ordered the Earl of Arundel to attend this unfortunate princefs to Cologne; where, having languifhed to the following year, in a condition very unfuitable to her high birth and former dignity, fhe died about five months before the implacable Cardinal. This poem was addreffed to the

Queen in the year 1638, in the thirty-third year of Mr. Waller's age.

The conclusion of this poem will be best understood by those who are acquainted with the Gierusalemme Liberata, in the nineteenth book of which the combat of Tancredi with Argantes, and in the twentieth that of Rinaldo with the Soldan, is described; and it needs no greater recommendation to be read, than its having been reverenced by Mr. Dryden next to the Æneis of Virgil. Mr. Waller not only learned the art of versifying from Fairfax's translation of it, but the subject made a lasting impression on his maturer judgment; for in some of his latest compositions, as well as in this, he expresseth a desire that the Christian princes would enter into a religious confederacy to rescue the holy sepulchre from the hands of the Infidels. In this place it will not be improper to give a short account of the life of his favourite author.

Torquato Tasso was born at Sorrento, an ancient city in Italy, about six leagues distant from Naples, in the year 1544. In his infancy he manifested an amazing genius, which was afterwards cultivated at Rome and Padua with variety of polite literature; and when he was no more than twenty-two years old, he began to write his immortal Gierusalemme Liberata. Alphonsus Duke of Ferrara invited him to reside in his court, whither he repaired, and was received more like a victorious hero than a recorder of their actions; and, during his stay, was honoured with very singular marks of the Duke's esteem and affection. Nor was he less caressed by Charles IX. when, leaving Ferrara, he attended the Pope's nuncio to the court of France, which seemed to rival Italy in admiring him. But, to close these gaudy scenes, Fortune kept a dismal cataftrophe in referve; for Taffo, on his return to Italy, was unfortunately engaged in a duel, occafioned by a real or pretended amour, in which the reputation of a great lady was attainted; whereupon he was feized and imprifoned by the Duke of Ferrara's command, in whofe palace the challenge was given. In his confinement he was dejected into a deep melancholy, which terminated in ftupidity; in which fad difguife Montaigne tells us he faw him, bnt, without affigning the real caufe, imputes it to the violent career of fpirits which his great vivacity of wit had occafioned. " What a condition," fays he, (as Mr. Cotton makes him fpeak) " through his own " agitation and promptnefs of fancy, is one of the " moft judicious, ingenious, and the beft-formed fouls " to the ancient and true poefy, of any other Italian " poet that has been for thefe very many years, lately " fallen into ? Has he not great obligation to this vi- " vacity that has deftroyed him ? to this light that " has blinded him ? to this exact and fubtle appre- " henfion of reafon that has put him befides his ? to " his curious and laborious fcrutiny after fciences

O ij

" that has reduced him to a brute? I was more angry
" (if possible) than compassionate, to see him at Fer-
" rara in so pitiful a condition survive himself; for-
" getting both himself and his works, which (with-
" out his knowledge, though before his face!) have
" been published deformed and incorrect."** The
ingenious translator thought his author in this place
had described Ariosto, a very pardonable mistake!
since many flights in his Orlando seem to have been
the dreams of an over-heated imagination. I cannot
find how long Tasso continued in this deplorable condition; but, it is said, by the care that was taken of
him in an hospital, he recovered the use of his reason,
and Thuanus informs us, that in his lucid intervals
he wrote like one inspirited with a divine fury, and
was master of a judgment sedate and cool enough to
correct what he composed. At last he was invited to
Rome to receive the laurel, with the public solemni-
ties with which it is usually conferred in that city;
but whilst the pageantry was preparing, he was seized
by a fever, and died in the fifty-first year of his age;
and being privately interred in the church dedicated
to St. Humphrey, a plain marble was laid over his
grave, with this epitaph; *Hic jacet Torquatus Tassus*;
where, some years after, Cardinal Bevilaqua erected
a handsome monument, with a Latin inscription,
longer, indeed, than the former, but so unequal to the
person it commemorates, that it is not worth my
transcribing.

The country, to my Lady of Carlisle, p. 6.

THE Lady Lucy Percy, whom the beſt Engliſh poets of that age, and Voiture, the politeſt wit of France, celebrated under the title of The Counteſs of Carliſle, was a younger daughter of Henry Earl of Northumberland; who, who upon a ſuſpicion of his not having been entirely ignorant of the gun-powder plot, was for many years impriſoned in the Tower. During his confinement the Lady Lucy was married to James Hay, created Viſcount Doncaſter, and Earl of Carliſle, by K. James I.; with which alliance her father was ſo highly offended, that with extreme difficulty ſhe obtained his forgiveneſs, but could never regain his affection. In conjunction with a wonderful vivacity of wit, and all the graces peculiar to her ſex in a moſt eminent degree, ſhe was bleſſed with a maſculine vigour of mind, but is cenſured for having abuſed it to the perplexing King Charles's affairs with the parliament; on which account a late learned and ingenious writer calls her, " the Helen of her country." But here it will be more decent to draw a veil over her political errors, and view her only in that agreeable light in which Mr. Waller and Sir Toby Mathews have placed her. The latter of theſe gentlemen has given us her deſcription in proſe, which is alluded to by Sir John Suckling in his Seſſion of the Poets. I only ſay it is alluded to, but believe it was originally mentioned; for I am perfuaded that, in the verfe on which I ground my conjecture, for the word *care*, we fhould read,

For had not her Character furnifh'd you out
With fomething of handfome, &c.

A fmall number of Suckling's plays were printed for himfelf, to prefent to the quality when they were acted at court; but his poems and letters were publifhed by his friend the Earl of Denbeigh after his death, from fuch imperfect copies as his Lordfhip could haftily collect; and therefore it is not ftrange if many of them ftill retain their original corruption. In the poem I have juft quoted (to inftançe in no more) Shillingfworth, Walter, Cid, have been conftantly mifprinted for Chillingworth, Walker, and Sid, *i. e.* Sidney Godolphin. But it is time to let the character itfelf atone for this digreffion which it occafioned.

" This lady's birth is noble, from a high and an-
" cient defcent, and in it her blood is kept pure by
" often alliance with great and princely families. Time
" has allowed it a line of longer meafure than almoft
" to any by continuance, and fo, as we cannot with
" cafe give an account of the firft greatnefs and eleva-
" tion of her anceftors; but yet it leaves certain marks
" by which we may (as by a kind of back-light) point
" at many of them, whofe courage and virtues have
" dignified both their good fortunes and their ill.

" She is of too high a mind and dignity not only to
" seek, but almost to wish, the friendship of any crea-
" ture; they whom she is pleased to chuse are such as
" are of the most eminent condition both for power
" and employments; not with any design towards
" her own particular, either of advantage or curiosity,
" but her nature values fortunate persons as virtuous;
" who, if they be not so by this opinion, they have
" an advantage of them who are so, by this choice:
" It may be she doth this by way of gratitude to For-
" tune, who hath taken so much care of her, as that
" from a doubtful, and, I might say, a kind of fear-
" ful, condition, she hath placed and secured her; as
" it were, in her own very arms; from whence this
" great lady might yet, perhaps, have removed her-
" self by the careless use of those benefits, of the pro-
" visions which Fortune hath made for her, were they
" not too abundant. They who are even as it were
" in her very veins, as brothers and sisters, she ex-
" tremely loves, but she values them more as they are
" so to her; she wants not also kindness for their
" children. But such as are more removed from her
" she considers no otherwise than as streams, which
" run too far to have any participation of her excel-
" lencies. She has as much sense and gratitude for
" the actions of friendship as so extreme a beauty will
" give her leave to entertain; and from our sex she
" may expect all expressions of servitude by the very

" nature and duty thereof. She more willingly allows
" of the converfation of men than of women; yet
" when fhe is amongft thofe of her own fex, her dif-
" courfe is of fafhions and dreffes, which fhe hath
" ever fo perfect upon herfelf, as fhe likewife teaches
" them by feeing her. Amongft men her perfon is both
" confidered and admired, and her wit, being moft
" eminent among the reft of her great abilities, fhe
" affects the converfation of the perfons who are moft
" famed for it; though yet fhe be fo handfomely
" civil to all, as that at the firft you would believe
" her to be more guided by that civility of her's
" than perhaps fhe is, fince fhe will rather fhew what
" fhe can do, than let her nature continue in it; un-
" lefs fhe confider fomething in the perfons very ex-
" traordinary and new, which fhe cannot find by their
" admiring her, (for that is not to be avoided !) and
" then fhe may requite them by allowing it : but yet
" if even that be not expreffed with the affiftance of
" fortune, and when fhe is in a good humour, and in
" the diftance and with the duty for which fhe looks,
" you may perhaps find fcorn when you expect accep-
" tation; reproving more the omiffions of (that which
" the majefty of her perfon teaches) reverence, than
" fhe cherifhes (what her beauty both begets and en-
" forces) love : yet will fhe freely difcourfe of love,
" and hear both the fancies and powers of it; but if
" you will needs bring it within knowledge, and bold-

" ly direct it to herself; she is likely to divert the dif-
" course, or, at least, seems not to understand it; by
" which you may know her humour and her justice;
" for since she cannot love in earnest, she would have
" nothing from love, so contenting herself to play
" with Love as with a child. She hath too great a
" heart to have naturally any strong inclination to
" others, not allowing them to grow from thence, as
" finding there no motions of affection, but only up-
" on consideration of the merit of others towards her:
" so that naturally she hath no passion at all, since
" inclinations are the ground and foundation upon
" which passion is built: but yet she will observe them
" whose reputation gives a value to their persons and
" condition, as if she would not be unwilling to find
" something of entertainment whereby to please her-
" self, or pass her time. But then, her examinations
" going ever by way of compulsion towards herself,
" they return unsatisfied. I conceive her not to be of
" a less sensible nature than she will acknowledge in
" herself. I believe she cannot find in it those little
" tendernesses which she will disallow in others, but
" yet, upon occasions worthy of her kindness or com-
" passion, (which, though they differ in their nature,
" yet they agree in the same shews) it hath broken
" out sometimes like suppressed flames: but I confess
" they are so few occasions that can bring it thus to
" light, as she may well be mistaken in her own heart

" by the seldom working of it; or, peradventure, in
" her reason she may make it this defence against
" those expreffions, that they are occafions to force
" her to take this unfenfiblenefs upon her nature,
" which is like giving of denials before suits be asked,
" or else as proclamations which forbid what may
" happen; and then, if they be disobeyed, it is to
" to be upon our own peril. She affects particular so
" much, that she diflikes general courtefies, and you
" may fear to be less valued by her for your oblig-
" ing her; she, peradventure, believing it to proceed
" in them from some eafinefs and cuftom of the
" mind, rather than from a generofity and humanity
" of the nature; which I conceive to be her greatest
" injustice, having obferved her to be so careful for
" some who have defired favours from her, as that
" her charity or her nature bath fought advantages
" for them who were ftrangers to her; who yet might
" well have taken them from those other who were
" not so to her. To shew her underftanding, not
" her difvaluing, of perfons, she will freely deliver
" her opinion of them; and as, in whomfoever we
" can speak of, there is, for the greatest part, more
" to be reformed than commended, fo, in the deli-
" vering of her cenfures that way, it shews her judg-
" ment can difcover (that which we ftrive moft to
" conceal) our imperfeétions and errors. Though she
" be obferved not to be very careful in the public exer-

" cifes of our religion, yet I agree not with their opi-
" nion who hold her likely to abandon and change
" it, not only for the faith and truft which fhe hath
" in the truth and goodnefs of it, but to avoid the
" doing of that which fhe believes to be a levity and
" declaration of a former ignorance. This lady, whom
" both Fortune and Nature have ever been in ftrife
" to ferve, (the one with her benefits, the other with
" her blefings) wants not a fenfe and contentment
" in both ; but conveniences of this kind being no
" true delight, fhe takes the greateft joy in the per-
" fections of her own perfon, fince Fortune cannot
" give her fuch a ftore and ftock as Nature doth to
" all that behold her; from which you may yet, per-
" haps, come to take fo much that you may find it to
" be a burthenous treafure, fince you cannot lay it
" out, or make any ufe of it, fhe being not to be pur-
" chafed by her own gifts. If gratitude may be pro-
" cured from her, it may go for an extraordinary re-
" ward, though from others it would be held but for
" a cold charity. She is more efteemed than beloved
" by her own fex in two refpects; the one, for that
" her beauty far exceeds theirs, and the other, for
" that her wit doth the like; which makes moft of
" them (efpecially fuch as pretend towards either of
" thefe excellencies) to avoid her company through
" their envy, as being conftrained in it, her beauty
" putting their faces out of countenance, as her wit

" doth their minds. She is so great a lover of varie-
" ty, as that when she may not otherwise exprefs
" it, she will remove her own thoughts, if not change
" her opinions, even of thofe perfons that are not
" leaft confidered by her; and when they have given
" her this entertainment, let them settle again in their
" former places with her. She hath certain high and
" elevated thoughts in which she is pleafed moft, and
" they carry her mind above any thing within her
" knowledge. She believeth nothing to be worthy of
" her confideration but her own imaginations: thefe
" gallant fancies keep her in fatisfaction when she is
" alone, where she will make fomething worthy of
" her liking, fince in the world she cannot find any
" thing worthy of her loving. Amongft the reft of
" her unnumbered perfections, she hath a grace and
" facility, (and I might well fay, a felicity) in her
" expreffions, fince they are certain, and always in
" the beft and feweft words: and as they are hand-
" fome, they are likewife fo faithful in the relation
" of any thing, as that she refines the language, and
" yet within the true limits of the occafion, adding
" nothing to the fubftance, but yet infinitely by the
" manner. She is in difpofition inclined to be chole-
" ric, which she fuppreffes, not, perhaps, in confide-
" ration of the perfons who occafion it, but upon a
" belief that it is unhandfome towards herfelf; which
" yet, being thus covered, doth fo kindle and fire her

3

" wit, as that, in very few words, it says somewhat
" so extracted, as that it hath a sharpness, and strength,
" and taste, to disrelish, if not to kill, the proudest
" hopes which you can have of her value of you. She
" affects extremes, because she cannot suffer any con-
" dition but of plenty and glory, in which, if she had
" not an assured and very eminent kind of being, she
" would fly to the other extreme of retiredness, and
" so rather obscure herself than not be herself; it be-
" ing natural to her, as her life, to maintain it in
" magnificence. She hath been told by her physi-
" cians, that she is inclined to melancholy ; and this
" opinion of theirs proved to be the best remedy for
" it, by the mirth which she expressed at it. This I
" say to shew her to be of a cheerful nature in her
" own opinion, who best can judge of it, as she, the
" most comely of all creatures, can express it. She
" hath, as all noble hearts have, ambition, which, I
" conceive, she rather conserves as a humour necessary
" to the mind, (as those of the body also are) than
" for any particular end or wish, she being so free
" from the want of any thing, as that it must be a
" study (and in that a pain) for her to inquire what
" to desire."

All that remains to be added concerning this celebrated lady is, that she had no children by the Earl
of Carlisle, whom she survived, without engaging in
a second marriage, to the year 1660; and was then in-

terred, near her unfortunate father, at Petworth in
Suffex.

To my Lord of Northumberland, on the death of his Lady,
p. 8.

I cannot with any certainty inform myfelf in what
year the lady died who occafioned the writing this
poem, and will defer my conjecture till I come to fix the
date of that which immediately fucceeds. She was the
Lady Anne Cecil, daughter of that Earl of Salifbury to
whom chiefly the old Earl of Northumberland im-
puted the lofs of his liberty; and when he was told,
in the Tower, what choice his fon, the Lord Percy,
had made, he expreffed his abhorrence of the marriage with this paffionate exclamation, " My blood
" will not mingle with Cecil's in a bafon." I can add nothing, and nothing needs to be added, to that amiable character which Mr. Waller has left of this lady;
and therefore I will proceed to tranfcribe the Earl of
Clarendon's account of her lord, which is far from being equally advantageous to his memory.

    " Of thofe who were of the King's council, and who
" ftaid and acted with the parliament, the Earl of Nor-
" thumberland may well be reckoned the chief, in re-
" fpect of the antiquity and fplendour of his family, his
" great fortune and eftate, and the general reputa-
" tion he had among the greateft men, and his great

" intereſt by being High Admiral of England. Tho'
" he was of a family that had lain under frequent
" blemiſhes of want of fidelity to the crown, and his
" father had been long a priſoner in the Tower, un-
" der ſome ſuſpicion of having ſome knowledge of the
" gun-powder treaſon ; and after he was ſet at liber-
" ty by the mediation and credit of the Earl of Car-
" liſle, (who had, without and againſt his conſent
" married his daughter) he continued to his death
" under ſuch a reſtraint, that he had not liberty to
" live and reſide upon his northern eſtate. Yet this
" lord's father was no ſooner dead than the King
" poured out his favours upon him in a wonderful
" meaſure. He begun with conferring the Order of
" the Garter upon him, and ſhortly after made him
" of his privy council. When a great fleet of ſhips
" was prepared, by which the King meant that his
" neighbour princes ſhould diſcern that he intended
" to maintain and preſerve his ſovereignty at ſea, he
" ſent the Earl of Northumberland admiral of that
" fleet, (a much greater than the crown had put to
" ſea ſince the death of Queen Elizabeth) that he
" might breed him for that ſervice before he gave
" him a more abſolute command : and after he had
" in that capacity exerciſed himſelf a year or two,
" the King made him Lord High Admiral of Eng-
" land ; which was ſuch a quick ſucceſſion of boun-
" ties and favours as had rarely befallen any man

" who had not been attended with the envy of a fa-
" vourite. He was in all his deportment a very great
" man, and that which looked like formality was a
" punctuality in preferving his dignity from the in-
" vafion and intrufion of bold men, which no man
" of that age fo well preferved himfelf from. Tho'
" his notions were not large or deep, yet his temper
" and refervednefs in difcourfe got him the repu-
" tation of an able and a wife man; which he made
" evident in the excellent government of his family,
" where no man was more abfolutely obeyed, and
" no man had ever fewer idle words to anfwer for;
" and in debates of importance he always expreffed
" himfelf very pertinently. If he had thought the
" King as much above him, as he thought himfelf
" above other confiderable men, he would have been
" a good fubject; but the extreme undervaluing
" thofe, and not enough valuing the King, made him
" liable to the impreffions which they who approach-
" ed him by thofe addreffes of reverence and efteem,
" that ufually infinuate into fuch natures, made
" in him: fo that after he was firft prevailed upon
" not to do that which in honour and gratitude he
" was obliged to, (which is a very peftilent corrup-
" tion!) he was with the more facility led to concur
" in what, in duty and fidelity, he ought not to have
" done, and what at firft he never intended to have
" done; and fo he concurred in all the councils which

" produced the rebellion, and ftaid with them to
" fupport it. ' ' " He died in the year 1668, *anno ætat.*
" 66, and was buried, near his·fifter, the Countefs of
" Carlifle, at Petworth, having been the tenth Earl
" of his family, and the fixth who had been honour-
" ed with the Garter."

To my Lord Admiral, of his late ficknefs and recovery, p. 10.

The time and occafion of writing this poem appears to have been when the Earl of Northumberland
was appointed General of the Englifh army againft
the Scots, and excufed himfelf from action by pre-
tending want of health, though his conduct foon afterwards evidenced it was want of inclination to exert
that vigour which the King's affairs required, and
which, of all men living, he was the moft bound by
gratitude to have exerted : and therefore we may
fuppofe that Mr. Waller made him the compliment
of thefe verfes, (a very feafonable one to cover his
difaffection) in the latter-end of the year 1640, *anno
ætat.* 35. And the death of the Earl's lady being mentioned as if it were ftill green in his memory, the pre-
ceding poem was probably written the year before,
or perhaps a little earlier.

To Van Dyck, p. 13.

Sir Anthony Van Dyck was born at Antwerp, in the
year 1599, and gave fuch early proofs of his moft ex-

cellent endowments, that Reubens his master, fearing
he would become as universal as himself, to divert him
from histories, used to commend his talent in painting after the life, and took such care to keep him
continually employed in business of that nature, that
he resolved, at last, to make it his principal study. For
his improvement he went to Venice, where he attained the beautiful colouring of Titian, Paulo Veronese,
&c.; and after a few years spent in Rome, Genoa,
and Sicily, returned home to Flanders, with a manner of painting so noble, natural, and easy, that Titian himself was hardly his superior, and no other
master in the world equal to him for portraits. He
came over into England soon after Reubens had left
it, and was entertained in the service of K. Charles I.
who conceived a marvellous esteem for his works,
honoured him with knighthood, presented him with
his own picture set round with diamonds, assigned
him a confiderable pension, sat very often to him for
his portrait, and was followed by most of the nobili-
ty and principal gentry of the kingdom : but towards
the latter-end of his life he grew weary of the continued trouble that attended face-painting; and being
ambitious to immortalize his name by some more glorious undertaking, he went to Paris, in hopes of being employed in the grand gallery of the Louvre: but
not succeeding in that design, he returned to England, and made a proposal to the King, by his friend

Sir Kenelm Digby, to form Cartoons for the Banqueting-houfe at Whitehall, the fubject of which was to have been the Inftitution of the Order of the Garter, the Proceffion of the Knights in their habits, with the ceremony of their Inftalment, and St. George's feaft: but his demand of 80,000 *l.* being thought unreafonable, whilft the King was upon treating with him for a lefs fum, the gout and other diftempers put an end to that affair, and his life, 1641, in the forty-fecond year of his age, and his body was interred in St. Paul's. He was low of ftature, but well-proportioned, very handfome, modeft, and extremely obliging; a great encourager of all who excelled in any art or fcience, and generous to the very laft degree. He married the daughter of the Lord Ruthven, Earl of Gowry, one of the greateft beauties of the Englifh court, and lived in ftate and grandeur anfwerable to her birth. His own garb was generally very rich, his coaches and equipage magnificent, his retinue numerous, his table very fplendid, and fo much frequented by people of the beft quality of both fexes, that his apartments feemed rather to be the court of a prince than the lodgings of a painter. *See Mr. Graham's Lives of the Painters.*

To my Lord of Leicefter, p. 15.

" The Earl of Leicefter was a man of great parts, very
" converfant in books, and much addicted to the ma-

" thematics; and though he had been a foldier, and
" commanded a regiment in the fervice of the States
" of the United Provinces, and was afterwards em-
" ployed in feveral embaffies, as in Denmark and in
" France, was in truth rather a fpeculative than a
" practical man, and expected a greater certitude in
" the confultation of bufinefs, than the bufinefs of this
" world is capable of; which temper proved very in-
" convenient to him through the courfe of his life.
" He was, after the death of the Earl of Strafford,
" by the concurrent kindnefs and efteem both of
" King and Queen, called from his embaffy in France
" to be Lieutenant of the kingdom of Ireland, and in
" a very fhort time after unhappily loft that kind-
" defs and efteem : and being, about the time of the
" King's coming to Oxford, ready to embark at Chefter
" for the execution of his charge, he was required to
" attend his Majefty for farther inftructions at Ox-
" ford, where he remained: and though he was of
" the council, and fometimes prefent, he defired not
" to have any part in the bufinefs, and lay under
" many reproaches and jealoufies which he deferved
" not; for he was a man of honour and fidelity to
" the King; and his greateft misfortunes proceeded
" from the ftaggering and irrefolution in his nature."
Earl of Clarendon's Hiftory, Book VI.

To my young Lady Lucy Sidney, p. 18.

The title of this poem is reprinted here as I find it
in the first edition of Mr. Waller. The lady to whom
it is addressed was the Lady Dorothy's younger sister:
she was born in the year 1625, and married to Sir
John Pelham, grandfather to his Grace the present
Duke of Newcastle.

To Amoret, p. 19.

I remember to have heard his Grace the late Duke
of Buckinghamshire say, that the person whom Mr.
Waller celebrated under the title of Amoret was the
Lady Sophia Murray.

To my Lord of Falkland, p. 23.

In the beginning of the year 1639, (when Mr. Waller was in the thirty-fourth year of his age) King
Charles was obliged to raise an army to oppose the
Scots in their intended invasion of England, and appointed the Earl of Holland, brother to the foremen-
tioned Earl of Warwick, to be General of the Horse,
which proved of fatal consequence to his Majesty's
service: for he no sooner brought the troops within
view of the rebels, but he made a most shameful re-
treat, and left his courage, conduct, and fidelity, to
be questioned by all men, as their passions or interests
inclined them to censure. " He was a very well-bred

" man, and a fine gentleman in good times, but too
" much defired to enjoy eafe and plenty when the
" King could have neither, and did think poverty the
" moft infupportable evil that could befal any man
" in this world." And by that bafe maxim he was
probably fwayed, after he had received many unme-
rited favours, to abandon his royal benefactor when
he moft wanted his fervice. But his ingratitude was
feverely revenged upon him by the very party to which
he revolted; and too late endeavouring to redeem the
reputation of loyalty, he fell, unpitied, a facrifice to
the fame faction for which, not many years before,
he had too wantonly proftituted his honour. In that
inglorious northern expedition, which occafioned the
writing this poem, he was accompanied by that great
ornament of human nature Lucius Carey, Lord Vifcount Falkland, who about four years afterwards was
flain at the battle of Newbury; " a perfon of fuch
" prodigious parts of learning and knowledge, of that
" inimitable fweetnefs and delight in converfation,
" of fo flowing and obliging a humanity and good-
" nefs to mankind, and of that primitive fimplicity
" and integrity of life, that if there were no other
" brand upon this odious and accurfed civil war than
" that fingle lofs, it muft be moft infamous and exe-
" crable to all pofterity." *Earl of Clarendon's Hiftory,*
Book VII.

To *Chloris, p.* 29.

CHLORIS! *since first our calm of peace,* &c.] I never had
the least suspicion that this little poem was not ge-
nuine, before I found this memorandum annexed to
the title of it in the table of an old edition, " which
" Mr. Waller says is suppositititious, in an edition given
" my father, (out of which I transcribed the additions
" into this) faultily printed, but corrected by the Au-
" thor under his own hand." After all, the verses are
written so exactly in Mr. Waller's manner, and I not
being able to inform the reader to whom this book
formerly belonged, I suppose he will think himself at
liberty to believe, that our Author wrote them when
he was young, and afterwards was too delicate to own
them under the title which they bear in the first impression,—*To Chloris, upon a favour received.*

To *Mr. William Lawes, &c. p.* 31.

HE was master of the public and private music to
K. Charles I. by whom he was distinguished with marks
of particular esteem, and usually called The Father of
Music. In the Great Rebellion he preserved his duty
and gratitude inviolate, and was slain in the quarrel
of his royal master at the siege of Chester, in the year
1645. All the best poets of that age were ambitious

of having their verfes compofed by this incomparable artift; who, having been educated under Signor Coperario, introduced a fofter mixture of Italian airs than before had been practifed in our nation.

. .

To his worthy friend Sir Thomas Higgons, upon his tranf-lation of the Venetian Triumph, p. 38.

THE Venetian Triumph was a poem compofed by Gio. Francefco Bufenello, addreffed to his friend Pietro Liberi, inftructing him to paint the famous fea-fight between the Turks and Venetians near the Dardanelles, in the year 1656; which Thevenot, who was at Conftantinople during the action, has defcribed in the fifty-third chapter of the firft book of his Travels. This method of addrefs was afterwards imitated by Mr. Waller, in his poem on the Duke of York's victory over the Dutch, and continued long the prevailing mode, both in panegyric and fatire, till one of our poets difgraced it fo effectually, by degrading it from the pencil to Vanderbank's loom, that it will require a writer of Mr. Waller's genius and authority to bring it again into fafhion among us. I cannot think, after all Bufenello's compliments, that Liberi ever attained to any diftinguifhing excellence in his art, fince I do not remember that he is mentioned among the moft eminent mafters of the Venetian School. Befides this poem, Bufenello compofed two dramatic baubles, the fubftance of which are Poppæa and Statira, which were acted by the *Virtuofi Cantanti* at Venice; to the latter of which there is prefixed a proteft, which, becaufe it is fhort, and gives us an idea of the writer, I will here tranflate : " The au- " thor protefts that every word and phrafe relating " to the Diety, *viz.* gods, idols, idolatry, ftars, hea- " ven, deftiny, chance, and fuch others, are purely " the flights of his pen, to adorn his poefy, and give " ftrength to his diction : in other refpects the fame " author, who writes like a poet, adheres religioufly " to the faith and practice of a Chriftian."

To a friend, of the different fuccefs of their loves, p. 39.

THE title of this poem in the firft edition is, " To " A. H. on the different fuccefs of their Loves ;" which initial letters were probably intended for Alexander Hambden, a relation of our Author, who engaged with him in that confederacy which is commonly called Mr. Waller's Plot; and though, perhaps, his name pre- ferved him from being profecuted with the fame fe- verity as others, yet the parliament fuffered him to die in prifon, though no judgment had been given a- gainft him, for; " the tender mercies of the wicked " are cruel."

To Zelinda, p. 40.

THE Author feems to have compofed thefe verfes purely for an exercife of his fancy, upon reading the fixth book of Des Maretz's Ariane; where Palamede addreffing his courtfhip to Zelinde, who was defcended from the Parthian kings, fhe anfwered, " I am a prin-
" cefs, and being fuch, I will liften to propofals of
" this kind from none but a prince." Upon this the gallant takes fire, and the dialogue grows fo warm, that, as himfelf obferves, it looked as if he came to affront the princefs, rather than to infinuate himfelf into her affections. Mr. Waller being probably of opi-nion that Monfieur Palamede's arguments were too *brufque* to be advanced in a difpute with a lady, who numbered not fewer than twenty kings of her proge-nitors, wrote this poem in a more tender and courtly ftyle, which I leave to be compared with Des Maretz's profe, by thofe who are inclined to decide the prize of gallantry between them.

To my Lady Morton, &c. p. 42.

ANNE Countefs of Morton was daughter to Sir Ed-ward Villiers, (the great Duke of Buckingham's bro-ther) and wife of Robert Douglas Lord Dalkeith, who, on the death of his father, fucceeded to the Earl-dom of Morton. She was one of the moft admired beauties of that age, and the graces of her mind were not inferior to those of her person; for which reason she was distinguished by the concurrent choice of King Charles I. and his Queen, to be governess to the Princess Henrietta, whom she conveyed, in disguise, from Oatlands into France, in the year 1646. At that time Mr. Waller was there in exile, and to his private calamities had a large addition of sorrow, in seeing that coast covered with the wrecks of a royal family, which, but a few years before! he had beheld in so flourishing a security, that one might have reasonably believed the greatest violence of Fortune would have beat on it in vain. And very disproportionate to their affliction and former grandeur was their reception at the court of France, through the artifice of that poor-spirited politician Mazarine; who, though he was a member of the Sacred College, seems to have reverenced Cromwell more than his Maker. But, having first observed that Mr. Waller presented these verses to the Lady Morton, *anno Dom.* 1650, *ætat.* 45, I will dismiss this unpleasing subject with Cardinal de Retz his account of a visit which he paid at the Louvre, as it is told by his translator. * * * " I went to visit " the Queen of England, whom I found in her daugh-" ter's chamber, who hath been since Duchess of Or-" leans. At my coming in, she said, " You see I am " come to keep Henrietta company; the poor child " could not rise to-day for want of a fire." The truth

" is, that the Cardinal, (Mazarine) for fix months
" together, had not ordered her any money towards
" her penfion ; that no trades-people would truft
" her for any thing, and that there was not at her
" lodgings in the Louvre one fingle billet.* * * I re-
" membered the condition I had found her in, and
" had ftrongly reprefented the fhame of abandoning
" her in that manner, which caufed the parliament
" (of Paris) to fend 40, 000 livres to her Majefty."
Pofterity will hardly believe that a princefs of England, grand-daughter to Henry the Great, hath wanted a faggot, in the mouth of January, to get out of
bed in the Louvre, and in the eyes of a French court!

A panegyric to my Lord Proteßor, &c. p. 45.

Upon the detection of Mr. Waller's defign to pro-
mote the King's fervice in the City, (of which the
Earl of Clarendon has given a large account in the
feventh book of his Hiftory of the Rebellion) White-
locke informs us, that " he obtained a reprieve from
" General Effex; and after a year's imprifonment
" he paid a fine of 10,000 *l.* was pardoned, and tra-
" velled into France ;" where, having continued for
about ten years, upon his friends' application to Cromwell, who had then folely engroffed the inflaving of
the nation, he was permitted to return ; and about
the year 1654, *anno ætat.* 49, he expreffed his gratitude to the Ufurper in this admirable panegyric.

To the King, upon his Majefty's happy return, p. 53.

—THE date of this poem coincides with the fifty-fifth year of Mr. Waller's age, from which time his genius began to decline apace from its meridian : yet, whatever traces of old age may appear in his latter compofitions, (as Longinus fays of Homer) we muft ftill confcfs it to be the old age of Mr. Waller.

* * * Cognofcite, Teucri !
Quae fuerint Illi juvenili in corpore vires.

We are told in the *Menagiana*, that when he prefented this poem to the King, his Majefty faid, he thought it much inferior to his panegyric on Cromwell. " Sir," replied Mr. Waller, " we poets never " fucceed fo well in writing truth as in fiction."

To the Queen, upon her Majefty's birth-day, &c. p. 57.

QUEEN Catharine, Infanta of Portugal, was born on the 14th of November, *N. S.* 1638, but her birthday was obferved in England on the 25th of that month, agreeable to the old method of computation ; on which day Mr. Waller prefented this poem to her Majefty, foon after her recovery from a dangerous fever, *anno Dom.* 1663, *atat. fua* 58.

This poem concludes that edition which was printed in the year 1664, at which time Mr. Waller ex-

preſſed his reſolution to hang up his harp, by ſub-
ſcribing theſe two verſes from Horace. *lib.* i. *ep.* I.

Nunc itaque et verſus, et caetera ludicra pono;
Quid verum, atque decens curo, et rogo, et omnis in hoc ſum-

But ſince he ſoon relapſed into poetry, I thought it
would not be very material to preſerve them any
longer in their uſual ſtation. It appears, from the date
in the title of this poem, that Mr. Waller wrote and
preſented it to the Queen, *anno æt.* 78.

To the Ducheſs of Orleans, &c. p. 59.

THE Princeſs Henrietta Maria, youngeſt daughter of
K. Charles I. was born at Exeter on the 16th of
June 1644. When ſhe was about two years old ſhe
was privately conveyed into France, as hath already
been obſerved in the Remarks on the poem to the
Counteſs of Morton; where, ſoon after the reſtoration, ſhe was married to the French king's only brother, Philip Duke of Anjou, who ſucceeded to the
title of Orleans on the death of his uncle. But, alas!

Eumenides tenuere faces de funere raptas,
Eumenides ſtravere torum. • • •

She is ſaid to have been extremely beautiful; and
even Burnet confeſſeth that ſhe was thought the wit-
tieſt woman in France, though ſoon afterwards, re-
penting of his ingenuity, he takes ſome pains to poi-
ſon her reputation. Being prevailed upon by the

French king to endeavour to engage her brother, King Charles II. in a league with him to humble the Dutch, she arrived at Dover about the middle of May 1670, where she staid something more than a fortnight, and was entertained by all her royal relations, attended with the flower of the English court, with all possible demonstrations of joy, during which time a scheme against Holland was concerted. Her husband, while she was absent, either wrought upon by the weakness and malice of his own nature, or the wicked insinuations of others, contracted an ill opinion of her conjugal virtue, so that nothing but her blood could extinguish his jealousy; and accordingly, soon after her return to St. Cloud, she was dispatched by a dose of sublimate given her in a glass of succory-water, when she had just completed the twenty-sixth year of her age. During her torments, which for about ten hours were violent, she expressed great resignation, and told the Duke of Orleans, that " she was the willinger to " die, because her conscience upbraided her with no- " thing ill in her conduct towards him." After such a declaration of her innocence, made in the very article of death, it ill became a Christian bishop to impeach her fidelity. Mr. Waller writ this poem, *anno ætat.* 65.

SONG.

Stay, Phœbus! stay, p. 67.

THE famous Philip de Mornay was a favourite and privy counſellor to Henry IV. of France, till that monarch revolted to the Romiſh communion, from whom, I ſuppoſe, the lady to whom this ſong is addreſſed was deſcended and ſhe probably was one of Queen Henrietta's attendants, who, upon the miſbehaviour of Madame St. George and the Biſhop of Mende, were obliged to quit both the Engliſh court and kingdom, in the year 1627; but this I offer purely as a conjecture of my own, and refer it to the reader's diſcretion to receive or reject it. The latter ſtanza of theſe verſes (which are certainly of Mr. Waller's earlieſt production) alludes to the Copernican ſyſtem, in which the earth is ſuppoſed to be a planet, and to move on its own axis round the ſun, the centre of the univerſe. Dr. Donne and Mr. Cowley induſtriouſly affected to entertain the fair ſex with ſuch philoſophical alluſions, which, in his riper age, Mr. Waller as induſtriouſly avoided.

EPIGRAMS, EPITAPHS, AND FRAGMENTS.

Epigram upon the golden medal, p. 81.

THE title of this epigram is ſo conciſe, that it renders the concluſion of it almoſt as obſcure as any paſ-

fage in Perfius or Lycophron. I am very diffident in
advancing a conjecture fo much in the dark; yet for
once I will venture, in hope that, fince it is offered with
caution, it will be rejected with candour if it is not
approved. Roti, the celebrated graver to K. Charles II.
was fo paffionate an admirer of the beautiful Mrs.
Stuart, (afterwards Duchefs of Richmond) that on
the reverfe of the beft of our coin he delineated the
face of Britannia from her picture; and in fome medals,
where he had more room to difplay both his art and
affection, the fimilitude of features is faid to have
been fo exact, that every one who knew her Grace,
at the firft view could difcover who fat for Britannia.
This epigram, therefore, compliments the Duchefs
upon her virtue being impregnable, and fuperior to
temptation; in which fenfe, whatever effect it may have
upon our faith, it is reconciled to our underftanding.
And, if I may be indulged in carrying my conjecture
a little farther, I fancy thefe verfes were compofed
foon after Roti had ftamped that medal, the date of
which is coincident with the fixtieth year of Mr. Waller's age.

Epitaph on Colonel Charles Cavendifh, p. 86.

This gallant gentleman was a younger fon of William Earl of Devonfhire, and brother to that beautiful and every-way-excellent Lady Rich, who hath already been mentioned. His genius led him equally to

excel in letters and in arms; but the courfe of his ftudies (in which the mathematics engaged his principal attention) being interrupted by the rebellion, he was among the firft who drew their fwords in the crown's defence; and after many fignal fervices performed for the King in the North, he was flain at Gainfborough, 1643, in the twenty-third year of his age. Cromwell, who commanded that party of rebels by which he was defeated, in a letter to the Committee of Affociation then fitting at Cambridge, fays, "My captain-" lieutenant flew him with a thruft under the fhort " ribs:" which may very well confift with another account, which informs us that he was murthered in cold blood, after quarter had been offered, and he had accepted it. His body was then depofited at Newark, but removed, and buried with his mother's at Derby, in the year 1674.

Early abroad he did the world furvey, &c.] The Memoirs of the family of Cavendifh inform us, that after this gentleman had made the tour of France and Italy, he embarked at Venice for Conftantinople; and, after a long circuit by land through Natolia, failed to Alexandria, thence to Cairo, vifited Malta in his courfe to Spain; and from Spain returning to Paris, he arrived in England about the end of May, in the year 1641.

Epitaph on the Lady Sedley, p. 88.

SHE was Elizabeth, only daughter of the learned Sir Henry Savil, Provoft of Eton College, and wife to Sir John Sedley, a Kentish Baronet, by whom she was mother of that SirCharles who so fairly diftinguished himself among the politeft wits in the court of K. Charles II.

Epitaph to be written under the Latin infcription, &c. p. 89.

CHARLES HOWARD, Lord Vifcount Andover, was eldeft fon to Thomas Earl of Berkfhire, whofe child, for whom this epitaph was intended, lies interred in New-Elm church, in the county of Oxford, from whence I have received the Latin infcription referred to in the title, which is fuch a wretched compofition, and the chifel has mangled it fo much in the pointing and fpelling, that I can make no other ufe of it but only to difcover, by this noble youth's having died in the year 1641, that Mr. Waller feems to have written thefe verfes before he was banished, and probably in the thirty-feventh year of his age.

OF DIVINE LOVE.

THE Divine Poems were the laft of Mr. Waller's productions, moft of them having been written when he was about eighty years old : in which, though there is not the fame elevation and fire as in his earlier compofitions,

His setting sun still shoots a glimm'ring ray,
Like ancient Rome, majestic in decay.   Mr. Dryden.

And thus I have endeavoured to discharge the debt
of gratitude which I owed to Mr. Waller's memory
for the pleasure I have received in reading his Poems,
by attempting to restore the text to its original purity, and adding such illustrations as some of them very
much wanted. They are extended, I confess, to a
much greater length than I designed; yet I am very
sensible that many defects are remaining, which I shall
be glad to see supplied, as I wish the whole had been
undertaken by some abler hand, having a far stronger
inclination to please and improve myself with the
writings of others, than to trouble the world with my
own. In the great variety of persons and things of
which these Observations consist, some, but I hope no
very material, errors may have escaped me; as I find,
upon a hasty review, in the article relating to Mr.
Lawes, (p. 31.) that not he, but his elder brother William *, was favourite musician to K. Charles I. and
slain by the rebels at Chester: for next to the uncom-
mon felicity of committing no mistakes, it is surely
the most generous pleasure to confess and correct
them.

* This gentleman's name is so printed in the title to the
poem.

5

CONTENTS.

Page

OBSERVATIONS

On the following Poems, excerpted from Mr. Fenton's edition of Waller in the 1729.

Page

From the APOLLO PRESS,
by the MARTINS,
Sept. 15. 1777.

THE END.

www.ingramcontent.com/pod-product-compliance
Lightning Source LLC
Chambersburg PA
CBHW020626030726
47497CB00007B/2430